His kiss was warm, drugging her senses

"Damn," Jed muttered softly. "Liza—"
She hated his calm, controlled voice.

"Please," she whispered. "I don't want to talk."

"A few minutes ago you called me contemptible
and disgusting." His low voice was cynically
amused. "Am I supposed to feel honored now
that you want me to make love to you?"

"Don't be cruel," Elizabeth murmured, shame
creeping in to steal her pleasure.

"I'm sorry, Liza," he said in a gentler yet firm
tone. "I thought I'd stopped wanting you, but
I haven't. The bitterness hasn't gone, either,"
he ended grimly.

"I don't understand." She gazed at him
bewilderedly.

"I know you don't." The glint in his eyes was
ruthless. "Maybe someday...." He was
withdrawing from her, emotionally as well as
physically. "Good night, Elizabeth."

JANET DAILEY AMERICANA

Janet Dailey
Americana

THE WIDOW AND
THE WASTREL

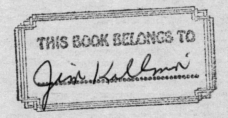

THIS BOOK BELONGS TO

Jim Kallman

Harlequin Books

TORONTO • NEW YORK • LONDON
AMSTERDAM • PARIS • SYDNEY • HAMBURG
STOCKHOLM • ATHENS • TOKYO • MILAN
MADRID • WARSAW • BUDAPEST • AUCKLAND

The state flower depicted on the cover of this book is scarlet carnation.

Janet Dailey Americana edition published November 1987
Second printing September 1988
Third printing September 1989
Fourth printing September 1990
Fifth printing November 1991
Sixth printing July 1992

ISBN 0-373-89885-1

Harlequin Presents edition published November 1977
Second printing March 1980
Third printing April 1981

Original hardcover edition published in 1977
by Mills & Boon Limited

THE WIDOW AND THE WASTREL

CHAPTER ONE

ELIZABETH CARREL stepped through the door of her home, a tennis racquet tucked under her arm. it was another hot August day. The heat and exertion had combined to leave her feeling drained and exhausted as she leaned tiredly against the hardwood door.

'Elizabeth, is that you?' The mature, feminine voice held an authoritative ring.

Pushing the thick, raven-black hair away from her face, Elizabeth straightened away from the door, the vulnerable look leaving as her canvas shoes carried her farther into the brick-tiled foyer.

'Yes, Rebecca,' she answered, not bothering to glance into the priceless antique mirror hanging on one wall of the entryway.

At the archway into the living room, she paused, her green eyes gazing at the smart, sophisticated woman within. Perfectly styled silver-gray hair gleamed from beneath a summer hat of blue flowers, an exact match to the opaque flowered dress of pale blue, impeccably tailored to show off the slender form of the much older woman. A brooch of amethyst and sapphires was the only jewelry. A bone-colored handbag to go with the bone-colored shoes sat on an oak table.

'I thought you would have left for your luncheon by now,' Elizabeth commented.

'I would have,' Rebecca Carrel replied. The melodic smoothness of her tone carried a hint of censure. 'But I sent your daughter to her room an hour ago to get ready for her music lesson and she hasn't come down yet. Perhaps you will see what's keeping her.'

Elizabeth smiled wanly at her mother-in-law. 'I'll see.'

The stairway leading to the upper floor of the old home was in a hallway of the foyer. Her shoes made little sound on the hardwood steps, the patina of many years adding to their high polish. At the door to her daughter's room, Elizabeth paused and knocked once.

The action brought a curious smile to the full curve of her lips. It hadn't been prompted by a reluctance to enter Amy's room without permission, but by a silent demand that the formal atmosphere of the house made. After a grumbling acknowledgment from the room, she entered.

There was an understanding light in her eyes as Elizabeth looked at the sullen figure staring out the window. Rebellion was outlined in the erect frame and squared shoulders.

'Hello, Amy.'

The cap of curling brunette hair turned at her mother's voice, brown eyes snapping with displeasure. 'Mother, do I have to have my lesson today? Can't I miss it just once? If I was sick you wouldn't make me go.'

The impulse was there to agree, but Elizabeth held it

back, and walked farther into the room. Her daughter was rebellious enough as it was without adding impetus to her fight.

'I think you'd better have your lesson today. There will be other days when you'll have to miss because of some special thing that's planned,' she reasoned.

'I'll bet,' Amy pouted openly.

'Your grandmother's waiting for you downstairs.'

'I know.' The admission was made through gritted teeth. 'I just hate these lessons, Mother! Mrs. Banks keeps making me do the same thing over and over and over. And that fan keeps making horrid noises and it's so hot.'

'I thought you told me that you liked playing the piano.' Elizabeth prompted gently, a smile held in check at the vehemence in her daughter's voice.

'I like playing the piano, but I don't like lessons and practising those stupid scales!'

'In order to do one, you have to do the other.'

'Oh, Mom!' Amy sighed.

The reverting back to the less formal mode of address signalled the agreement of her daughter. This time Elizabeth didn't hold back her smile, but let the warmth of her love show through as she tilted up the downcast chin.

'You'd better get your music books and get downstairs or your grandmother will be late for her luncheon,' she ordered lightly.

'The sooner I go, the sooner I can leave,' Amy sighed again, widening her eyes with mock adult resignation.

7

'Such enthusiasm!' Elizabeth laughed softly and pressed a quick kiss on her daughter's forehead before pointing her in the direction of the door.

She didn't follow Amy down the stairs, but remained at the top of the landing near the door to her own room staring after the youthful form going down the steps. She was a beautiful child who would be an even more beautiful adult. Unconsciously Elizabeth marveled that this exquisite little human being had come from her flesh and blood. She had long ago ceased to remember that Amy's father had played any part in the creation.

When Elizabeth stepped into her room, the photograph on the dressing table reminded her. The man in the picture was a stranger to her. Their marriage had been of such a short duration when he was killed in an automobile accident. At the time, she hadn't even known she was carrying Amy. It was difficult to remember she had ever been married, so brief had been their interlude together.

Of course, she had been married to Jeremy Carrel or she wouldn't be living in his family's house today. And Amy resembled her father with her dark brown hair and eyes, but her attitude and personality was totally dissimilar to his. Jerry, who had never been a mother's boy, had accepted the role his family played in the community, society, business, and leadership. When Elizabeth had married him, he had been marking time and preparing for the day when he would take command of the Carrel law firm and its holdings from his father. Never once did he strain at the invisible bonds of what was socially acceptable as Amy did. He never did anything in excess except what was accepted.

Turning away from the photograph, Elizabeth saw her reflection in the full-length mirror standing freely in the corner of her room in its self-supporting oak frame. Her tennis whites accented the gleaming bronze shade of her shapely legs, slimly rounded hips curved into a slender waist, then the line curved back out to indicate the adult fullness of her breasts. She didn't need the reflection to tell her that she was a beautiful woman, hardly looking old enough to have an eight-year-old child.

Perhaps, Elizabeth decided as she turned from the mirror to remove her tennis clothes, Amy's stubborness did come from her father's unshakable determination. And from her own as well. She simply hadn't been able to steer Amy's self-will into a constructive outlet. The minor rebellions seemed to have increased in the last year. Elizabeth wondered if the lack of a male figure in her daughter's life was the cause.

Amy's grandfather, Jerry's father, had been taken from them quite suddenly with a heart attack almost two years ago. He had never spent much time with Amy even though they lived in the same house. Nor had Amy ever indicated any great affection for her grandfather, but sometimes Elizabeth found it difficult to know exactly what was on her daughter's mind.

Hesitating in front of the open door of her closet, she shrugged away the thought of dressing and reached instead for the cotton caftan. Its loose-fitting folds would be much more comfortable on this hot, stickily humid day.

Downstairs again, Elizabeth paused in the roomy, old-fashioned kitchen long enough to fix herself a cold glass of lemonade. She had already had a light lunch with her tennis partner and friend, Barbara Hopkins. Besides, with the house quiet, this was the perfect time to read through the plays the local theatre group was considering using this season.

Although there was no longer a Carrel in the business community, Rebecca Carrel had not relinquished her leadership in the other areas. Elizabeth had the impression that now that her husband was gone, her mother-in-law actually enjoyed being the sole center of attention, no longer needing to share the spotlight with her husband. It was a mean thought since Elizabeth knew at first hand how devoted Rebecca had been, always the perfect wife, the perfect helpmate and the perfect confidante to her husband, while maintaining her own social position and never allowing the two to conflict.

Rebecca Carrel was a marvel of organization and Elizabeth had learned considerably from her. Now she played an active role in the 'right' social clubs of the community. She was a Carrel, and the younger set sought her out in much the same way as her mother-in-law. Her life was full to the point that there was rarely an empty moment. Maybe that was why she never missed Jerry as much as she thought she would. In the beginning, Rebecca had not allowed her the time to grieve, although Elizabeth had felt more shock than grief. Then there had been Amy. And now — well, now there was now.

As she entered the living room, Elizabeth stopped and, with a smile, walked to the piano in th e small alcove. She ran her fingers lightly over the ivory keys, remembering her own young rebellion at practising scales. Amy seemed to have an aptitude for the piano, expressing an enjoyment similar to what Elizabeth had known. Certainly she had never pushed Amy into learning.

Setting her lemonade glass down, she began experimentally picking out the melody of a song. More memories came flooding back as the nimbleness of her fingers increased. It was at the piano recital that she had met Jerry. He had come with his parents and they had been introduced for the first time at the reception that followed the recital.

Not that Elizabeth hadn't known who he was all the time. She doubted that anyone in the county hadn't known Jeremy Carrel. Nearly everyone had given up expecting that he would marry a local girl. When she had seen that admiring light in his dark eyes, she knew there was hope. If she played her cards right, Elizabeth had realized that she could catch the most eligible bachelor around — and in truth, that was exactly what she had set out to do. It had been terribly easy to let herself fall in love with Jerry.

Mary Ellen Simmons, the aunt who had raised Elizabeth after her parents had died when she was eleven, had not entirely approved of the marriage. She had insisted that at seventeen Elizabeth couldn't possibly know that she wanted to spend the rest of her life with Jerry Carrel, fearing that her niece was more impressed with his background than in love with the individual. Her suspicions were never proved one way or the other. In fact, Elizabeth hadn't given them a thought until this minute.

Curious. Her fingers slipped into a slower, more pensive tune. Why was she suddenly dwelling on what happened so many years ago? She had never questioned before whether she had truly loved Jerry or not. It was a moot question that had no definitive answer.

A surge of restlessness burst through her for no apparent reason. Her fingers clanged on the keyboard, discordant and harsh. Anger turned inward that she had wasted time with useless daydreaming that could have been better spent studying the theater's plays.

Sliding to the edge of the piano bench, Elizabeth reached for her lemonade glass. With it safely in hand, she turned to rise impatiently and froze. A figure was leaning against the wooden frame of the living room archway.

A cold chill ran down her spine at the unkempt appearance of the man; a sweat-stained shirt of light blue was half-unbuttoned to accent a masculine chest tanned teak brown. Lean hips were covered by slacks that were probably a darker blue, only they were too dust-covered to be certain. The stubble of unshaven beard darkened the chiselled angles of his face. A windbreaker was over one shoulder and a much used duffle bag was sitting on the floor beside him. Thick, tobacco brown hair had been combed away from the tanned face by the fingers of one hand. Hazel gold eyes were watching Elizabeth with lazy intentness.

'What are you doing in here?' she breathed, suddenly conscious of how isolated the house was in its country setting.

'Is the concert over?' his deep, husky voice asked.

She rose to her full five feet six inches, making her shaky voice sound icy and imperious. 'You have no right to be in here. I suggest that you leave immediately before I contact the authorities.' There was a flash of white in the beard growth as the man smiled and remained where he was. 'If you're looking for a handout, you'll get none here. The highway is a half mile down the road. I'll give you five seconds to leave and I'm phoning the police.'

With the threat voiced, she walked to the telephone and picked up the receiver. Any second she expected him to pull a gun or knife and assault her.

'I didn't expect the fatted calf,' he drawled, 'but I did think I would at least be offered a meal.'

'You'd better leave.' She dialed the first digit, ignoring his comment.

'You're going to feel like a fool, little sister. It might be interesting to see a Carrel with a red face, even one claiming the name by marriage,' he chuckled softly.

For the second time, Elizabeth froze, her green eyes swinging back to the stranger in the archway, confident, not the least bit intimidated by her threat. She didn't know him, but he seemed to know her, or at least he was aware of her connection with the Carrels.

'Who are you?' she demanded. Her fingers were still tightly clenching the receiver.

'Have I changed that much in all these years?' A brow lifted in mock inquiry. 'I would have recognized you anywhere. I like your widow's weeds. Jerry always did like you in blue.'

The receiver nearly was dropped from her hand. 'Jed?' she whispered in disbelief.

'The one and only,' he confirmed, straightening from his slouching position against the door. 'Had you given me up for dead?'

'We haven't heard from you —' Elizabeth began, then stopped. 'Jed, your father — he had a heart attack almost two years ago. He's ... he's dead.' There seemed no way to put it less bluntly.

'The house hasn't changed much,' was his comment as his tawny gold gaze swept the room, then it returned to the sympathy etched on her oval features. 'I heard about Dad.' he said finally with little emotion visible on his unshaved face. 'Mother's letter caught up with me abᵒ·t a year ago. There seemed little point in returning bₒ ᵗhat time.'

'Why ... why have you come back?' she asked.

His tongue clicked in mock reproval. 'It's bad manners to ask probing questions, Liza.'

'Elizabeth,' she corrected automatically, and he laughed.

'Still striving for status, I see.'

'I don't like the name Liza. It sounds —'

'Common was the adjective I believe you used'

before,' he reminded her. 'It was shortly after you became engaged to my brother and you were trying to appear the poised and sophisticated young lady to impress my mother. You became very angry when I called you that in front of them.'

'I remember.' A tautness crept into her expression as she averted her eyes from the watchfulness of his.

'Where's Mother?'

'At a luncheon in town,' Elizabeth replied.

'Of course, it's Thursday, isn't it? I had forgotten that she holds court every Thursday.' A hard smile moved over his mouth, somewhat cynical and derisive.

'If you would like to clean up, the room at the end of the stairs is empty. You can put your things there. There are fresh towels in the bathroom.'

His expression didn't change. 'Is that a subtle hint that you find my appearance less than presentable?' Jed Carrel queried mockingly. 'It was a hot, dusty walk out here.'

'Do you mean you walked from town?' She frowned at him in surprise.

He glanced down at his dust-covered shoes and slacks. 'My feet were the only transportation available. The local taxi was no doubt ferrying Mother's lady friends to their weekly luncheon with the Queen.'

'You could have waited,' Elizabeth murmured automatically.

'I was anxious to see if Thomas Wolfe was right, that you can't go home again. So far I would say he's right. My old room at the head of the stairs is in use?·

'It's Amy's now.' She bristled faintly at his implication. They had met only once. They were virtually strangers, so why should he expect her to welcome him back with open arms?

'Amy?' Jed questioned with a dark brow arched in inquiry.

'My daughter.' Her chin lifted fractionally to a defiant angle.

Again there was the cynical movement of his mouth that was supposed to resemble a smile. 'Oh, yes,' he nodded. 'I remember Jerry left you with a child. Amy, that was my grandmother's name.'

'That was her namesake,' Elizabeth admitted.

'Mother must have liked that. Or was it her suggestion?'

His mocking jibe struck home, but Elizabeth wouldn't acknowledge it. 'Several names were discussed before Amy was born.' She turned away abruptly. 'Have you eaten? Would you like me to fix you a light lunch?'

'Breakfast, please,' he requested instead. 'I haven't adjusted to the time zones yet. For me, it's tomorrow morning. Omelette and toast will be fine.'

He was picking up his duffle bag and striding with catlike smoothness for the stairway door. Elizabeth stared after the lean, masculine figure. After almost nine years she couldn't be blamed for not expecting to see her husband's brother again, or for practically forgetting his existence. In the last few years, his name had only been mentioned once that she could recall, and that had been when Rebecca, his mother, had wanted to notify him of his father's death. Just once.

They had only received three cards from him that Elizabeth could remember, short little notes that had been postmarked in different foreign ports ranging from the Pacific Islands to South-east Asia. His name had almost been forbidden from the very first.

Naturally when Elizabeth had first met Jeremy, she had been aware that he had a brother, younger by little more than a year. Jed was a wild one, the gossips had said, expelled from schools and colleges, ignoring every edict and principle of social behavior that his family stood for.

Her only interest had been in Jeremy. The escapades of his brother were of little importance. If she had thought of him at all, it had only been a concern that she should approve of her as a future member of the family. She had always known in the back of her mind that if Jeremy's family didn't approve of her, there would be no marriage regardless of how much he had professed to love her.·

Unconscious of her actions, Elizabeth turned to the kitchen, caught up in the memories of the past, a trip backward that had already begun before Jed's sudden arrival. Now her thoughts focused on her single meeting with him.

It had occurred only a day or two after Jeremy had proposed. She had met his parents once, briefly at a dance he had taken her to at the country club. After his proposal, she had been invited to dinner. Elizabeth had been afraid it was very significant that Jeremy had not yet given her an engagement ring.

When they had arrived here at his house, she had been a bundle of nerves, terrified that she would do or say the wrong thing. Jeremy had offered little support, growing more silent with each step they had taken toward the door. His parents and Jed had been in the living room awaiting their arrival. The hostile atmosphere had almost smothered Elizabeth. She had been certain the silent animosity was directed at her. It was quite a while before she realized their censure was directed at Jed.

Initially he had been silent, not the silence of disapproval, but of cynical amusement. Although he had never uttered a word to confirm it, Elizabeth had the distinct feeling that his parents' approval or disapproval of the girl he wanted to marry would not have affected his decision and he found it amusing that Jeremy sought it so earnestly. At the time, Elizabeth had been angered that he couldn't understand the necessity for it.

Except for an initial greeting and an odd comment at the dinner table, Jed had not addressed any conversation directly to her. Not that she had cared. In fact, she had been glad that he hadn't singled her out for attention in case his parents' anger rubbed off on to her. There had been an inner sensation that he knew she had silently taken the side against him and knew why.

After coffee had been taken in the living room, a tiny voice had suggested that this was the time to make a discreet withdrawal and give Jeremy an opportunity to speak to his parents in private. The smile of approval that had flashed across Jeremy's face when she asked to be excused to freshen up had told her that the suggestion was a wise one.

She had fussed with her hair and make-up and lingered as long as she dared before venturing into the hallway, crossing her fingers that she wasn't returning too soon. Jed was in the hallway. Something in his manner had prevented Elizabeth from walking past him.

'So you're the angel of virtue that has captured my elusive brother,' he had murmured softly, almost mockingly. 'You look more like a dark-haired witch to me.'

Her nervousness had increased with her uncertainty how to reply to his comment. It was one of those horrible moments when no suitable response came to mind.

She had smiled weakly. 'Jeremy will be wondering where I am. Excuse me.'

The light touch of his hand on her arm had stopped her. 'Doesn't it bother you that they're in there deciding whether to allow you the dubious privilege of becoming a member of the Carrel family?' He had frowned.

'I wouldn't marry Jeremy without his parents' permission,' she had answered, her expression adding that to do otherwise would be insane.

'How old are you?' Unusual hazel-gold eyes swept her oval face and slender figure, inspecting her with swift appraisal.

'Seventeen. Quite old enough to know my own

mind I'm sure,' Elizabeth had asserted defiantly.

'And you're in love with the idea of becoming Mrs. Jeremy Carrel,' Jed had mocked.

'More than anything else I want to be his wife. I love him.'

'Yet you wouldn't marry him if my parents disapproved,' he scoffed.

'Of course not,' she had answered.

'I don't believe you really love him or you'd fight tooth and nail to have him instead of passively waiting for someone else to give the verdict as to whether you'll marry him or not.'

'It's my life and my decision and none of your business!' His cutting jibe prompted a stinging retort.

'Don't marry him, Elizabeth.' There was a hard, warning note in his tone. 'Don't get caught up in the so-called glamor of the Carrel name and make a mistake you'll regret.'

'Aren't you being premature?' she had asked haughtily. 'It's possible that your parents will disapprove of me.'

'Oh, they will approve.' A corner of his mouth curled cynically upward. 'My moralistic father sees you as pure and untouched and has investigated your background sufficiently to be certain there's not a breath of scandal attached to your name. Mother is glorying in the almost worshipful attention you've been paying her. She's already deciding that she can mold you into the type of daughter-in-law she wants, as subservient to her wishes as Jeremy is.'

'That's not a very nice way to talk about your

parents.' The elation she had felt at his initial statement that they would give her permission for the marriage was taken away by his sarcastic analysis of their reason.

'The truth is often unkind, Liza.'

'My name is Elizabeth.' Her dislike of him had increased when he shortened her name. 'I don't like nicknames. They're so common.'

'And Elizabeth is filled with all sorts of royal connotations, isn't it?' Jed mocked. 'Forgive me if I don't bow.'

'Forgive me if I find it hard to believe that you and Jeremy are brothers,' Elizabeth retorted acidly.

'Don't apologize for that. That's been a puzzle almost since the day I was born. All I've heard is why can't you be more like your brother.' Jed laughed with unconcealed bitterness. 'I make too many waves, but I don't intend to change. I'm not like Jerry. I'm not content to walk in my father's shadow. I'll blaze my own trail in life.'

'So you condemn Jeremy because he is joining your father's firm,' she replied coldly.

'Not if that's what he wants.'

'Do you question that he knows?'

'The same way that I question if you know,' he replied.

'I know exactly what I want. To marry Jeremy,' Elizabeth stated without qualification.

'Do you?'

His fingers closed over her chin and tilted it up. Her green eyes rounded in surprise as she stared into the

21

lean face bending closer to hers. The astonishment at his action was so complete that she had made not one word of protest nor attempted to draw away. Nor was she prepared for the hard, passionate possession of his kiss, the raging fire scorching through her veins. Inexperience had held her frightened by what was happening. When the bruising pressure had been lifted, Elizabeth had only been able to stare into the satisfied gleam of his gold-flecked eyes, reminiscent of a cat playing with its prey.

'I doubt that Jeremy has ever kissed you like that, Liza,' Jed had smiled mirthlessly. 'His emotions are too severely checked to permit it.'

"'I certainly hope not,' Elizabeth had whispered breathlessly, a frightened pulse throbbing in her throat.

She and Jeremy had kissed many times. Warm satisfying exchanges they were, too. But never had she been left with the sensation that she was about to be seduced.

'Jerry r-respects me too much to treat me like that,' she had added in a more forceful voice that was still quivering slightly.

'Is that what you want from him? His respect and the Carrel name?' He was laughing at her youth, but she was powerless to stop it. 'He will be making love to you, you know.'

'But with gentleness and consideration.' A flush began creeping into her cheeks at his open discussion of such an intimate subject.

'I hope some day, Liza, you'll be honest enough to

tell me if that's what you really want.' He had sounded almost sorry for her.

'How dare you speak to me like this? How dare you treat me this way?' she had demanded, now angry that he thought she should be pitied.

'You've got to wake up, little Liza. Jeremy isn't the man for you,' Jed had pointed out smoothly, showing amusement at her display of temper.

'What's going on here?' Jeremy was visibly bristling at the end of the hallway, his dark eyes looking accusingly at Jed and Elizabeth.

With a guilty start, she had pulled away from the hand that was curled along the side of her neck in an obvious caress. She had been frightened that Jeremy would misunderstand and think she had invited this accidental meeting with his brother.

'I was just coming in —' she had begun to explain, but Jed broke in calmly.

'Yes, she was,' he agreed, 'but I waylaid her before she could hurry back to the safety of your side. I wanted to be the first to kiss your official bride-to-be. I didn't want her to have any doubts that I would welcome her into the house with open arms.'

The suggestive emphasis Jed placed on the last brought a stormy thundercloud into Jeremy's expression. Elizabeth had sensed that Jed was deliberately goading him into anger.

'You keep away from Elizabeth, Jed,' Jeremy had growled.

'Then congratulations are in order.' Jed turned to Elizabeth, who was still too paralyzed to move and smiled. 'The verdict is in and the sentence is about to be life. I wouldn't expect much mercy if I were you, Liza. The Carrel family isn't a forgiving lot — I know from first-hand experience.'

'Elizabeth, come here,' Jeremy ordered crisply.

As she started to walk by Jed, she read the silent message in his hazel gold eyes, repeating again that she was making a mistake. Her reply was to practically run to Jeremy's side, letting his arm circle her shoulders and draw her to him. She smiled into his face, seeing that her quick obedience had dulled the edge to most of his anger.

Then Jeremy's dark eyes had turned to his brother, standing alone several feet away, the expression in Jed's eyes shielded by half-closed eyelids.

'Mother suggested that for appearances' sake you should be the best man,' Jeremy had announced.

'I suppose I'm supposed to be honored to be included in the festivities at all. Do you think by giving me a major role that it will put me on my best behavior?' Jed had mocked.

'I've made my wishes known,' Jeremy had stated stiffly. 'I would like to have you as my best man. It's up to you to accept or refuse.'

Without answering, Jed had turned and walked away.

CHAPTER TWO

A FLASH of total recall brought vividly back to life that long-forgotten incident. Elizabeth's fingertips were unconsciously pressed against her lips. In retrospect, Jed's kiss did not seem nearly so frightening or unpleasant. The discovery was very unsettling because it was so at odds with her opinion of him.

Jed had not been best man at their wedding. In fact, a few days after her introduction to him, Jeremy told her that he had left for parts unknown. Although he had not added it, Elizabeth had sensed that Jeremy wished his brother Godspeed and a long journey. Secretly she had been surprised that his parents had endorsed the thought, but mostly she had felt relief that Jed would not be around.

In appearance, he and Jeremy had not resembled each other except for the brown hair. Jeremy had been an inch or two taller than Jed's six feet. His frame had been broader and more muscular in appearance than Jed's lean build. In Elizabeth's judgment, Jeremy had been the handsomer of the two, with a fine strong face that was youthfully manly.

At twenty-three there had been a chiseled hardness to Jed's features that the years had seemed to intensify, making him appear more cynical and rugged. Yet it had been his overpowering sense of maleness that had left Elizabeth feeling so naïvely insecure and inexperienced. She had known that she could become the kind of socially acceptable wife that Jeremy wanted, but the thought of Jed as her brother-in-law had filled her with trepidation. Then he had removed himself, taking with him her fear and uncertaintly.

Now Jed had returned. Why? It was a question without an answer, one that he had dodged successfully when she had asked him. If he had returned after Jeremy's death or his father's, Elizabeth would have understood. But there seemed little purpose for his return. She couldn't believe it was prompted by any sense of family loyalty or any driving desire to return to the home of his birth.

If it had been that, he wouldn't have returned looking like a common tramp, dirty and disheveled. No, if he had hoped to get back in good graces with his mother as the only remaining male member of the family, he would have made his homecoming in a more auspicious manner. He would have spent his last cent to look the part of a Carrel and not come walking across fields carrying a knapsack on his back, unshaven and unkempt.

'A penny for your thoughts — or is it more expensive to know what a Carrel is thinking?'

Elizabeth blinked into a pair of gold-brown eyes, catlike like the rest of Jed Carrel, always insinuating a lazy feline arrogance. She didn't have to be told it was a pose, that he could respond with catlike swiftness.

'They —' She took a deep breath to control the sudden acceleration of her pulse. 'They aren't worth a penny.'

'My omelette?' Jed prodded mockingly when she continued to stare at him.

'Right away.'

She turned quickly to the refrigerator, tearing her gaze from the transformation that had occurred in the space of a few minutes. The beard growth was gone, revealing a lean jaw and high cheekbones. The heady scent of some male aftershave lotion drifted around her nose. His tobacco brown hair gleamed a darker brown, courtesy of the shower spray; its natural waywardness even when combed properly giving him a more rakish appearance.

But again she had been struck by his maleness, her awareness awakened by the crisp, white, short-sleeved shirt only partially buttoned. The tanned skin of his bare arms rippled with sinewy muscles and the dark curling hair on his chest heightened the teak shade of his tan. His leanness made his strength seem primitively masculine. An inner sense told her that even when he was in formal clothing the impression would be just as strong.

It was difficult to work with her usual efficiency in the kitchen while his eyes watched her every move. Elizabeth forced herself to concentrate on what she was doing.

She glanced to where he sat straddling a kitchen chair to ask, 'Do you want your omelette plain or with cheese or ham?'

'Plain is fine,' Jed answered.

He waited until she had served his omelette and toast before making further conversation. 'Where's your daughter?' he asked.

'In town with Rebecca. She has a piano lesson shortly after noon.'

'Does she play as well as her mother?'

The question flustered Elizabeth. For an instant she found it difficult to assimilate that Jed was referring to her.

'Amy is just a beginner.' She reached for the coffee pot to pour herself a cup, uncaring of the hotness of the day's temperature. 'She's only been taking lessons for a little over a year. But she's quite good.'

'Does she look like you?'

Elizabeth didn't turn to the table immediately, but took her time adding a spoonful of sugar to the dark liquid. 'No, she takes after her father.'

'That's a pity,' Jed responded dryly.

'Why have you come back?' Her green eyes warily met the sliding glance of his.

'Do I have to have a reason?'

'Yes,' she breathed, letting him hold her gaze for what seemed an interminably long time before he returned his attention to the plate on the table. 'I can't believe you came back simply because this was your home.'

'Don't discount the pull of your childhood home. You can pull the roots out, but you always leave some behind,' Jed replied.

'Is that why you've come?' she asked, still not accepting the slightly ambiguous answer he'd come up with.

'That's why I've come here,' he agreed. 'But I think I returned to the States for a breath of civilization.'

'When will you be leaving?'

'Maybe tomorrow. Maybe never,' he shrugged, white teeth flashing as he bit into the slice of toast.

'I don't understand why you've come back now.' She brushed the raven hair away from her face, a tiny frown creasing her forehead.

'You probably don't even know why I left, do you?' The hard mouth moved into a wry smile.

'I know you argued with your parents,' Elizabeth hedged.

Jed pushed the empty plate towards the center of the table. 'All the time I was growing up it was one argument after another. Foolishly I kept believing that I could make my parents understand that all I wanted was to live my own life. When you and Jeremy became engaged, I'd been kicked out of three law schools. My father gave me the news that night that he had used his influence and money to get me accepted into another. He refused to accept that I didn't want to be a lawyer, that I wanted no part of the family business. A couple of days later I left.'

'I see,' she murmured.

'I doubt it.' His voice was coated with bitter mockery. It brought her head up sharply. 'Truthfully I didn't expect to find you here when I came back.'

'Where did you think I'd be?' Elizabeth laughed shortly in confusion.

'Married. You're a beautiful woman.' It was a

statement more than a compliment. 'I can't believe there haven't been offers.'

⸀ 'I haven't dated all that much since Jeremy died, and not with anyone on a regular basis.' Elizabeth turned her back on him, seeking to change the subject. 'Would you like some coffee?'

'Please.' When she set the cup before him, Jed asked, 'Why have you avoided seeing anyone regularly?'

'I haven't avoided it,' she answered sharply, responding to the hint of mockery in his tone. 'I simply haven't had a great deal of free time. A person doesn't when they have children.'

'Free time can be arranged if the desire is great enough,' he observed. 'Wasn't Jerry able to arouse a great enough desire?'

His jeering question jerked her chin up. 'We were very happy together,' Elizabeth stated with a frigid anger. 'Which is probably why I haven't been interested in anyone else.'

'Do you enjoy being the beautiful Carrel widow, challenging the men you meet to win your favors?' Jed inquired with biting softness. 'Or are you afraid that some man will show you how very inadequate Jeremy was?' His gaze slid to her mouth as if to evoke the memory of his kiss.

Elizabeth pivoted sharply away from the table, walking to the counter to set her cup down. 'Jeremy was very adequate and I have a daughter to prove it. Your questions are becoming much too personal and bordering on insolence.'

'The ability to procreate is not indicative of a man's prowess to arouse a woman's desires,' he laughed arrogantly. 'Was his respect and gentleness as satisfying as you thought it would be?'

'Yeṣ!' she flashed angrily.

'Honestly?' Jed prodded softly, and she realized he had come quietly up behind her.

'Yes, honestly,' Elizabeth declared firmly. A bitter anger rose in her throat. 'You haven't changed, Jed. I thought you were insulting and arrogant the first time I met you, and the years in between haven't altered that. You tried to turn me against Jeremy then and you're still doing it now when he isn't here to defend himself. I think that's disgusting and contemptible!'

'Seeing you again has brought back the memory of our first and only meeting, too,' he answered with serious thoughtfulness. 'You were an extraordinarily bewitching young creature, tantalizingly innocent and desirable. My mind tells me that you're mature and no longer innocent, but my eyes insist that you're still inexperienced. As a woman,' his voice became husky and caressing, 'you are even more desirable than you were as a girl.'

'Stop it!' She wanted to close her ears to his voice, but it was impossible.

'Looking back, part of the reason I left was you. That night I couldn't stop myself from kissing you, even though I knew I'd frightened you. I frighten you now, too.' His hands closed over the soft flesh of her upper arms. 'You're trembling.'

She closed her eyes to stop the quivering response at

his touch. 'From disgust,' she murmured wildly, needing to explain the reason for her disturbance.

'At least give me credit for leaving.' There was a smile in his voice. 'Had I stayed I probably wouldn't have been able to resist the temptation to make love to you, even if you were my brother's wife. Now —' Jed slid his hands down her arms, letting his fingers close around her slender wrists. Crossing her arms in front of her, he drew her shoulders back against his chest, 'Now I can hold you like this, bury my face in your silken black hair.' Elizabeth gasped in shock as he proceeded to let his action follow his words. 'And—'

'Let me go!' She tried to twist away from the sensuous nuzzling near her ear.

There was silent laughter in the warm breath that caressed her cheek and throat. Elizabeth discovered that Jed found her struggles amusing, aware that his superior strength would counter any attempt to be free.

'Elizabeth!' The startled and censorious voice came from the hallway door.

Flames of red burned her cheeks as Jed slowly released her, his tawny eyes laughing at her embarrassment as Elizabeth turned to face her mother-in-law. Jed did not turn immediately, keeping his back to his mother.

'Rebecca —' Elizabeth began, fighting to regain her composure and rid herself of the absurd sensation that she had done something to feel guilty about.

But she wasn't allowed the opportunity of identifying Jed as Rebecca Carrel broke in with haughty indignation, 'What were you thinking, carrying on like that, Elizabeth? What if Amy had come running here and seen you in the arms of this stranger? Who is this—'

'Hello, Mother.' Jed turned and spoke before she finished her slashing barrage of questions.

Rebecca's mouth snapped shut grimly, a finely drawn, charcoal eyebrow arching in something considerably less than overwhelming joy at her son's return.

'Your brother and your father have been in their graves for quite a while, Jed. Why have you bothered to come back now?' she asked shortly.

The firm line of his mouth thinned into a cold smile. 'I must have been drawn by your overwhelming motherly love,' he responded cynically. With negligent ease, he walked over and mockingly kissed her cheek.

'How long do you intend to stay? Or are you just passing through?' His mother's expression was still rigidly controlled.

'I haven't made any plans,' Jed shrugged, squarely meeting her dark gaze.

'I can believe that,' Rebecca agreed with cutting reproval. 'Your father and I did everything we could to prepare you for a decent role in life and you threw all of it aside, even the opportunity for a college education. You refused to plan, always insisting that you knew it all and refusing to listen to us. What has it gained you, Jed? You've hopped all over the Pacific and what do you have to show for it?'

The only indication Elizabeth saw which revealed

Jed's determined control of his temper was the slight clenching of his jaw. Otherwise he withstood his mother's tirade without any show of emotion.

'I haven't come back to argue whether what happened in the past was right or wrong, Mother,' he replied calmly. 'I guess I wanted to come back when I'd made my fortune.' He smiled in self-reproach. 'When I received your letter about a year after it was written and realized that Dad was gone, I knew I had too much of the same Carrel pride that I'd condemned. I've come home to make peace with you, Mother.'

Again there was the long, measured look between them. Elizabeth unconsciously held her breath, believing the sincerity in Jed's voice yet uncertain whether his mother did.

'You can have the room at the end of the stairs as long as you're here,' Rebecca said at last. 'Amy, Jeremy's daughter, has your old room.'

'Yes, Liza already offered me the use of the other room shortly after I arrived. I —' he glanced down at his fresh clothes — 'I needed to clean up after walking from town.'

'You *walked* from town!' his mother exclaimed in distressed anger. 'Did anyone see you? For heaven's sake, why didn't you take a taxi? What will people think if they saw you walking along the highway?'

'If anyone had seen me, they would probably have thought that I was on my way home,' Jed reasoned dryly.

'I wish you would be more conscious of our position

in the community,' his mother sighed rather bitterly.

At that moment, Amy appeared in the kitchen door-way having changed into an everyday outfit of shorts and top. Her gaze was immediately drawn to the stranger in their midst. Elizabeth realized it was probably the first time her daughter had seen a man in the house during the daytime since before her grand-father had passed away.

As she made her way to Elizabeth, Amy kept her curious brown eyes centered on Jed. There was no shyness in her silent appraisal, nor did she flinch from his returning look.

'Hello, Amy.' Jed's greeting was casual, not forcing any undue warmth or gladness into his voice.

Amy tilted her dark head back to look at Elizabeth. 'Who is he?' she demanded in a bold, clear voice that bordered on rudeness.

'Your manners, Amy,' Rebecca repremanded sharply.

Except for a stubborn tightening of her mouth, Amy pretended not to have heard her grandmother's reproval. Elizabeth had the fleeting thought that her daughter's slightly rebellious nature might have come from her uncle.

'This is your uncle Jed, Amy. He was your father's brother,' Elizabeth explained patiently.

Curiosity still remained the uppermost emotion as she turned her attention back to Jed. 'Hello,' she greeted him naturally. 'Did you know my father?'

'Yes, we grew up together,' Jed answered, calmly returning her intent scutiny of him.

'Did you know me when I was a baby?'

'No, I was on the other side of the world when you were born.'

His response did not impress Amy. 'I didn't know my father. He died before I was born, you know,' she informed him with marked indifference.

'I knew that,' he nodded.

'Did you like my father?'

'Oh, Amy, what a question to ask!' There was a brittle quality to the laughter Elizabeth forced through her throat, as she tossed a pleading look to Jed. 'He was your uncle's brother. Of course he liked him.'

'That's not exactly true,' he ignored her silent request to keep Jeremy's memory untarnished.

'Jed!' Elizabeth appealed to him angrily.

'He was my brother,' Jed continued with a faint smile grooving the side of his mouth. 'Because he was my brother, I loved him. But I didn't necessarily like him. Brothers tend to fight and argue a lot, Amy. Your father and I didn't agree on a lot of things.'

'What did you fight about?' Amy tilted her head interestedly to the side.

'That's enough questions, Amy,' Rebecca broke in coldly. 'Your uncle is probably very tired after his long journey and you're supposed to be practising the piano. Mrs. Banks told me you didn't do very well today, so from now on you'll practise an extra fifteen minutes at the piano every day.'

'Oh, Mother, no!' Amy made her angry protest to Elizabeth, frowning her appeal for the edict to be rescinded.

'You'd better do as your grandmother suggests,' Elizabeth answered quietly. 'If you do better at your next lesson, we'll consider eliminating the extra fifteen minutes.'

'Mrs. Banks is stupid,' Amy grumbled.

'I was going to swim in the pool after a while,' Jed inserted quietly, too quietly Elizabeth thought, 'Perhaps you can join me when you're finished with your practice, Amy.'

The frown was replaced by an immediate smile as Amy opened her mouth to heartily accept his invitation.

'I believe you've forgotten, Jed,' his mother spoke sharply, 'but in this house, there are no rewards or bribes for doing what you are supposed to do.'

With that parting shot, Rebecca Carrel pivoted around and left the kitchen. Seconds of heavy silence ticked by as Jed stared after her, yellow fire smoldering in his eyes.

'I'm sorry, Amy,' he said simply, turning back to the crestfallen child. 'Maybe another day.'

'Yes, maybe,' she sighed as if she didn't hold out much hope for that nebulous day to come. Her feet were dragging noticeably as she left the room.

'Nothing's changed,' Jed muttered bitterly beneath his breath.

Elizabeth knew the comment was not directed to her, but at his mother's insistence on strict discipline. Several times she herself had protested in Amy's behalf, but Rebecca's argument that it was for the good of the child always seemed a valid one. Besides,

Amy's spirit had never faded under the unbending rules of the house. In fact, Elizabeth was convinced it was the only way to keep her assertive personality under control. On her own she wouldn't have been as unwavering as Rebecca.

'Why are you living here, Liza?' Jed asked as she began clearing the dishes from the table. 'I'm certain the deaths of Jeremy and my father must have left you very well provided for.'

'They did,' she acknowledged, not pausing in her task as she replied. 'But this has been my home. And my name is Elizabeth.'

'What about the house you and Jeremy had? Wasn't that your home?' he countered.

'We only lived here after we were married.'

'Oh, my God!' he laughed in disbelief. 'You actually lived here — with my parents, after you were married! That must have given you a lot of privacy and time to get to know each other, with Mother for ever organizing your lives!' he jeered.

'It was only a temporary arrangement!' His mockery stung her into retorting sharply in defence. 'We had bought a house, but the whole place needed to be redecorated and furnished and the kitchen remodeled. It would have been foolish to try to live in it when it was in such a disorganized state.'

'Of course it never occurred to either of you to move into it and re-do the house in stages,' Jed offered dryly.

'Jeremy couldn't see the point in prolonging it. It was his decision to do it all at once and I agreed with him,' Elizabeth stated. 'Besides, he was working very hard for your father. It was only natural for him to want to come home to an orderly house at night.'

'What did you do all day?'

'If it's any of your business,' her chin quivered in anger, 'I was kept quite busy with the redecorating.'

'Under Mother's supervision, right?' he mocked.

Her eyes brightened with volatile temper to a more vibrant shade of green, contrasting sharply with the rich blue of her caftan.

'I was seventeen at the time and too inexperienced to handle such a formidable job on my own. I was very glad of your mother's assistance!'

'So the house was never completed?'

'Yes.' She turned away to the sink as she made the clipped response. 'We were to move into it, but Jeremy was killed in that car crash and I simply ... c-couldn't bring myself to live in the house that we were to share together.'

'So you stayed on here,' he said in a faintly accusing note.

'After I discovered I was pregnant with Amy, there was nowhere else for me to go. My aunt was in the hospital with a severe diabetes attack.'

'And Mother offered her assistance again, is that it?' Jed mocked harshly. 'When Amy was born, you were still young and inexperienced and knew nothing about babies, so you accepted her guidance again. You could have found a better teacher. In fact, you could have fumbled through on your own with the same results. A lot of women do, and without the benefit of the financial peace of mind you so luckily had.'

'You're so strong and so arrogantly confident that you know exactly what's right,' Elizabeth retaliated, 'that you probably don't know what it's like to feel lost and alone and frightened. I doubt if you know what it's like to need the support of someone else. I doubt if you know what it's like to need anyone!'

'Believe me, I need!' His voice vibrated huskily. 'If I didn't, I wouldn't have come home. Although it's some homecoming!'

'Don't blame me for that. You were the one who left! And three letters in nine years hardly sounds as if you were very homesick!'

'Do you want to know how many letters I received from my parents?' Jed flashed. 'Exactly two! One telling me of Jeremy's death and the other of my father's. My effort to keep the lines of communication open was not encouraged. I felt as if I was batting my head against a brick wall ten feet thick!'

'Then why did you come back?' she lashed out, angry that he was taking his frustration out on her.

'I've been asking myself that question ever since I arrived. I should have realized the age of miracles is over. I had thought,' the smile curving his mouth was turned inward in self-mockery, 'if I came back willing to make peace, my mother would meet me halfway, accept the way I am. The only thing she can allow herself to acknowledge is success.'

'That's a cruel accusation!' Elizabeth breathed in sharply.

His gaze glittered to her face, hard and unyielding

like a topaz sapphire. 'I love my mother deeply, but that doesn't make me blind to her faults.'

'What's wrong with being ambitious? Or wanting to better yourself?' she demanded.

'You've climbed to the top of this small social ladder. What do you think of the view? Is it what you expected it to be?' Jed countered. 'As fulfilling and rewarding as you thought?'

'Not fulfilling exactly, but that was a qualification Elizabeth made silently. 'All the activities keep me busy,' she defended. 'And I enjoy the charity work. It's very rewarding helping deserving people.'

'Deserving by whose standards? My mother's?' He punctuated the words with a short, derisive laugh.

'I think you've become harder and more cynical than she is,' Elizabeth observed.

'What about you? Are you becoming like her? Don't you think you'll ever desire the warmth and companionship of a man's love?'

'I haven't thought about it.' She was suddenly wary, not liking the subject change from his mother to her.

'Don't you think you would miss not having a man's arms around you again?' Jed continued his pursuit of the subject.

Her chin was raised upward to a defiant angle. 'I doubt it,' she replied. 'I was raised by a maiden aunt. Jeremy was killed so soon after we were married that I never really became accustomed to a man's attention. I think I can get along quite well without one.'

'Do you?' responded Jed with a faint challenge.

The instant he started walking toward her, Elizabeth backed away. Her defiant bravado was driven out by the sudden fear that he might try to test her assertion.

He stopped and chuckled softly. 'I was just going to get myself another cup of coffee,' he explained, letting his amusement show. 'Did you think I was going to challenge your statement and demand physical proof?'

'Earlier —' she began to remind him, with mistrust flashing in her eyes.

'What happened earlier was a fleeting impulse.' His expression was uncompromisingly hard. 'I may have said that I found you desirable, Liza, but I don't desire you. There's a vast difference. So you don't need to fear any unwanted advance. I don't intend to touch you again.'

Jed's statement was made so emphatically that Elizabeth was forced to believe him. His rejection of her as a woman was more of a blow to her self-esteem than she had thought. She should be rejoicing, but instead a strange depression was settling in.

'Don't you feel relieved, little sister?' His soft voice insinuated itself into her astonishment.

'O-of course.' She turned away, running a nervous hand through her ebony curls, pushing them behind her ear as she sought for her cool poise. 'Immensely so.'

'That's what I thought you'd say,' he murmured.

'Help yourself to the coffee. I have some work to do.' She avoided looking directly at him as she made her exit from the kitchen, grateful that she had the excuse of reading the plays to be alone for a while.

CHAPTER THREE

'PUT the roast at the head of the table, Elizabeth,' Rebecca instructed. 'Since Jed is here, he can carve it.'

As she started to transfer the platter of meat to the opposite end of the table, Jed appeared in the dining room archway. He was wearing the same white shirt and brown slacks as before.

'I'm honored, Mother, that you've put me at the head of the table,' he commented in a faintly derogatory tone, letting them know that he had overheard their conversation from the hallway.

'The eldest male Carrel always sits at the head of the table,' Rebecca responded curtly. 'In this case, it happens to be the only male Carrel.' Her dark gaze ran over his casual attire. 'We can delay serving for a few minutes while you change. I'm sure you must have forgotten that we always dress for dinner.'

'I hadn't forgotten.' Jed continued into the room, drawing the end chair where Elizabeth stood away from the table. 'Unfortunately I couldn't fit my white tie and tails into my duffle bag.'

'Don't exaggerate,' his mother snapped. 'A simple suit is sufficient.'

'There wasn't room for one of those either. You'll have to take me the way I am,' Jed stated, reaching for the carving knife and fork that Elizabeth had placed near the platter.

Rebecca pursed her lips together in displeasure, but said nothing in response. Waving an imperious hand at Elizabeth and Amy to be seated, she took the chair at the opposite end of the table from Jed.

'By the way,' he laid a perfectly sliced cut of meat on to Amy's plate, 'where's Maggie? Is this her day off?'

Maggie Connor had been a cook-housekeeper to the Carrel family for years, an almost permanent fixture in the house when Elizabeth had married Jeremy.

'She has retired. After your father died,' his mother explained. 'We no longer entertained, so there was no point in retaining her for just the three of us. Your father provided a generous annuity for her in his will and I let her go.'

'This meal looks very tasty,' Jed observed. 'Who does the cooking now? You, Mother?'

'Elizabeth does for the most part, although I occasionally lend a helping hand.'

Only Elizabeth knew how rare that helping hand was. Not that she objected. She preferred having the kitchen to herself.

'A Carrel who cooks?' The tawny gaze slid mockingly to her, dancing over her face when she quickly averted her green eyes. 'How did you learn such a skill, Liza?'

Elizabeth found it was difficult to respond naturally. She felt on the defensive and she didn't know whether to blame his taunting mockery or the hated abbreviation of her name. Perhaps it was simply an inability to feel at ease in Jed's presence.

'Actually I learned to cook as a child,' she answered stiffly. 'My aunt thought it was essential for me to learn, so I fixed a great many of our meals. After Jeremy and I were married, I naturally helped Maggie in the kitchen so I could learn how to prepare his favorite dishes. Later I simply helped out.'

'Maggie's age was beginning to show at last,' Rebecca inserted. 'She was becoming increasingly slow and haphazard in her work. It was best that she retired when she did.'

'Wasn't Maggie a year or two younger than you, Mother?' questioned Jed, a sharp glitter in his eyes.

'I really don't have any idea,' his mother bridled visibly.

'Do you do the housework too, Elizabeth?'

The faint emphasis he placed on her proper name made it even more difficult to tolerate than the nickname. 'Not all of it, no.'

'We have a young girl come in two or three times a week to take care of the general cleaning and the washing,' Rebecca explained.

'I like Mary,' Amy spoke up, adding in a faintly adult note. 'She's very nice.'

'Do the Reisners still own the farm down the road?' Jed asked.

'Yes, they do. You went to school with Kurt, didn't you?' His mother glanced up to receive his answering nod. 'He's taken over the farm from his father and his parents have moved into town. Why?'

'I thought I would stop over to see them tonight, that is,' there was a falsely courteous inclination of his tobacco brown head toward his mother, 'if you'll let me use the car.'

'There's a set of spare keys in the china cabinet,' she agreed.

Elizabeth had to restrain herself from audibly sighing in relief. She hadn't been looking forward to an evening of stilted conversation. Despite the appearance of polite discussion, the atmosphere between mother and son was decidedly hostile. Her own inclination was to avoid Jed as much as she could. He had delved too deeply into her personal life, asking questions that were none of his business and laughing at her answers. Arm's length was not a far-enough distance.

The instant the evening meal was over, Jed excused himself and left to visit their neighbors, the Reisners. He hadn't returned by the time Elizabeth went to bed some time after ten o'clock. Although she lay awake in the double bed for nearly an hour, she didn't hear him come back.

The next morning Elizabeth discovered the coffee was already made when she entered the kitchen. Breakfast dishes for one were washed and sitting in the draining board beside the sink. Rebecca didn't get up that early in the morning, so the dishes could only be Jed's. But there was no sign of him in the house nor in the yard surrounding the house.

Not until she returned to the kitchen to fix toast and juice for herself did Elizabeth find the note he had left under the bowl of fruit on the small dinette table. Her fingers crossed in a fervent wish that Jed had decided to leave as abruptly as he had arrived. The boldly firm handwriting informed her that he would not be back for lunch, but made no mention of where he would be in the interim.

If he had gone visiting, the only logical place he could have gone at this early hour of the morning was to the Reisner farm again, Elizabeth decided. She wasn't aware that he and Kurt had been close friends, but if they had gone to school together, it was possible. The few times she had seen Kurt, he had made no mention of it, although most of the townspeople had been reluctant to introduce Jed's name into a conversation.

Even though they were neighbors, Elizabeth didn't know Kurt that well. She knew he had been married at one time, but was presently divorced. That information she had gained from his sister Freda, who was a year or two younger than herself. She had liked Freda and would have seen her more frequently socially, except she had sensed that Rebecca would have disapproved of the friendship. Looking back, it seemed a weak reason for not pursuing the relationship. Elizabeth could well imagine Jed's contempt if he ever found out.

His opinion did not matter to her in the least, she reminded herself. She wished violently that he had never returned. Life had been very smooth. Now she was seeing all kinds of chuckholes in front of her. He was a disruptive influence that she had to learn to ignore to retain her own peace of mind.

'Good morning, Elizabeth.' Rebecca entered the kitchen looking youthfully fresh in a pink satin robe, her silvery blue hair carefully styled and light make-up adding color to her face. 'Is there any fresh grapefruit this morning?'

'Yes, I'll fix it for you.' Elizabeth slid back her half-eaten toast and walked to the refrigerator.

'I see Jed isn't up yet. I suppose he'll sleep until noon,' Rebecca sniffed her disapproval of such laziness.

'Actually he's up and gone.' She sliced the grapefruit in half and began running the knife along the skin of each section.

'How do you know that?'

'He left a note saying he wouldn't be back for lunch,' Elizabeth answered. 'He was considerate enough to wash up his breakfast dishes before he left, so he must have been up quite early.'

'Good,' Rebecca declared with a wide smile of satisfaction. It took Elizabeth a second to realize that she was commenting on his planned absence that morning rather than the fact that he had cleaned up after himself. 'You're going into town this morning, aren't you?'

'Yes, I have a committee meeting to see how the ticket sales are progressing for the charity dinner at the country club,' Elizabeth acknowledged as she set the grapefruit half in front of her mother-in-law.

Rebecca slipped a manicured hand into the pocket of her robe. There was a faint rustle, then she was handing a slip of paper to Elizabeth.

'While you're in town, I want you to stop by Shaw's Men's Store. I've made a list of things that Jed needs. The sizes are listed on the right,' Rebecca stated. 'I'm sure Fred will reopen our account.'

Elizabeth stared blankly at the paper. 'But how can you be sure these are the right sizes? I mean . . . wouldn't it be better to send Jed in himself when he comes back this afternoon?' She stammered slightly. -operate just to be obstinate. As for the sizes,' Rebecca paused, 'I've already checked to be sure they were correct.'

Glancing from the list to the woman delicately spooning out a grapefruit section, Elizabeth knew without a doubt that her mother-in-law had not questioned Jed. He would have been certain to guess the purpose.

'Do you mean,' she found the question she was about to ask distasteful, 'that you went through his things?'

'He doesn't even have a sports jacket.' Rebecca shook her head in arrogant disbelief. 'I didn't believe him last night. 'After the way he was raised, I was certain he had something decent tucked away in that disreputable bag, so I went through it last night while he was at the Reisners'. I hope he doesn't intend to get too friendly with them.'

For the first time that she could remember, Elizabeth took offence at the faintly snobbish ring in Rebecca's voice. 'They're very nice people,' she stated firmly.

Her mother-in-law's mouth opened to comment,

then she met the flashing defiance in the green eyes and appeared to change her mind. 'I suppose they are,' she agreed with marked lack of interest.

'Excuse me while I go to see what's keeping Amy,' Elizabeth murmured, moving away from the colonial style table.

'Be sure to put that list in your purse so you won't forget it,' Rebecca reminded her.

Fingertips curled around the paper, crackling it slightly. The impulse burned to hand it back to her mother-in-law with the retort to do her own dirty work, but Elizabeth held it back. The animosity in the air since Jed's return was beginning to affect her own outlook.

'I won't forget,' she promised, and walked from the room.

It was nearly noon when Elizabeth paused beside the store-front. The sign above the canopy read Shaw's Men's Clothing. She wished she hadn't left the cold lunch for Rebecca and Amy before leaving this morning. She would have welcomed an excuse to postpone this errand. Outside a few Christmas gifts for her father-in-law, she had never purchased any clothing for men. During her short marriage, Jeremy had always preferred to choose his own.

Nervously she ran her fingers along the scalloped neckline of her white sundress. Squaring her shoulders in determination, she walked to the door. A bell tingled above the door to announce her entrance.

The balding head of Fred Shaw, the owner, turned away from the customer he was helping to glance toward the door, and immediately he waved to his other male clerk to take his place as he excused himself to walk toward Elizabeth.

It flashed through her mind that this was usually the case. The owners or managers of the various stores in Carrelville invariably were the ones who waited on her, sometimes even letting other customers wait. It struck her suddenly as being very unfair.

'Good morning, Mrs. Carrel,' he greeted her. A wide, professional smile spread across his face while his eyes crinkled at the corners behind steel-rimmed glasses. 'It's going to be another hot one today, isn't it?'

'Yes, it is,' Elizabeth agreed, wondering if her vague embarrassment was revealed in her cheeks. 'If you're busy, Mr. Shaw, I don't mind waiting a few minutes.'

'Not at all, not at all,' he assured her quickly. 'I'll bet I can guess why you've called. I was just saying to my wife last night that we hadn't got around to buying tickets for your dinner. She suggested that I get a couple of extra so we can take our daughter and her husband along.'

'That's very generous of you, Mr. Shaw, but actually,' her smile faltered slightly, 'I stopped by to purchase a few items. Of course, I'll gladly sell you the tickets.'

Elizabeth knew that he was undoubtedly curious about who she was buying clothes for, but he didn't comment until the money and tickets had been exchanged.

'Now, what may I show you?' he asked, Elizabeth

took the list from her purse and handed it to him. 'This is almost a complete wardrobe.' He peered at her over the top of his glasses. 'Is the—er—rumor true that young Jed has come home?'

'Yes, Jed is back,' she admitted stiffly.

'For good?' Then as if he thought the question was too personal, Fred Shaw shrugged it aside. 'I suppose with Jed it's impossible to be certain.' He led her toward a rack of expensive dress suits. 'Craig Landers said that he thought he'd recognized Jed at the airport yesterday. The engine of Craig's small plane was being overhauled. That's why he was out there. Jed flew in, didn't he?'

Since Elizabeth hadn't asked, she could only assume that was so. 'I believe he did.'

'This is a nice one,' he suggested, removing a suit from the rack for her to examine. 'Craig mentioned that Jed looked a little worse from wear. Has he been ill?'

'Not that he mentioned.' Elizabeth guessed it was a reference to Jed's untidy appearance. 'Of course, he'd had a long journey. He was quite tired when he arrived at the house.'

'Where has he been? I heard once that he was on some South Pacific island.'

She fingered the material of a dark brown suit. 'He traveled a good deal,' she replied, remembering that the three letters had been postmarked at different places.

'What's he been doing all this time?'

That was another question that Elizabeth hadn't

thought to ask him. 'Various things,' she hedged.

'Jed never did seem the type to settle down to one thing. Never seemed the type to settle down at all.' Fred Shaw laughed as though he had made a joke. 'You probably never got to meet him. I think he'd already left by the time you became engaged to Jeremy.'

'He left shortly after our engagement was announced,' Elizabeth admitted, and tried to distract him from the subject by questioning him about the material in a particular suit.

Once he had answered that, Fred Shaw returned the conversation to Jed. 'Yes, I remember now. You and Jeremy were engaged before Jed left. We were all expecting Jed to come back for the wedding. 'Course, he never was one to follow convention. No, he wasn't dependable like his brother. Now Jeremy was a son that any parent would be proud to claim. He was a fine boy, trustworthy and a hard worker. But I guess I'm not telling you anything you didn't already know.'

'Jeremy was a very wonderful husband,' she murmured.

'His death was a real tragedy.' He shook his head and sighed. 'It's always the hardest thing to understand why somebody like Jeremy is taken. He could have done so much good for the community. Jed was always the irresponsible, reckless one with his devil-may-care attitude. I remember when he was barely in his teens he'd disappear for a day or two, then show up and claim he'd hitch-hiked to Dayton to see the Air Force Museum. Heaven only knows where he truly went. That was one boy who brought more than his share of heartache to his parents. They tried so hard to see that he had all the advantages that Jeremy had. Mr. Carrel refused to stop trying to get him a university education. Every time Jed was expelled, his father would be out looking for another place that would take him, paying whatever money was necessary. It was a shame, truly a shame.'

'That was all very long ago, Mr. Shaw,' Elizabeth said coldly.

Lost in his thoughts, as he was, it took several seconds for her reprimand to penetrate the store-owner's thoughts. By then it had lost some of its strength.

'Yes, it was a long time ago,' Fred Shaw agreed. 'After losing both Jeremy and Franklin, your mother-in-law is probably relieved to have a man around again.'

Nodding crisply in agreement, Elizabeth began selecting dress and sports outfits from the rack. She was fully aware that the instant she left the shop the news would spread all over town that Jed was back. The subtle barrage of questions she had endured led her to believe that Rebecca had sent her so that she wouldn't have to answer them initially.

Choosing quickly and unerringly, Elizabeth unconsciously picked out styles that would complement Jed's lean virility and not attempt to cloak it in formal, sophisticated designs. It was a relief when the list had been filled and the clothes carefully folded in boxes. She signed the charge ticket with a flourish, anxious to be gone before Fred Shaw's curiosity burst to the surface again.

Her car was parked at the end of the block. Elizabeth walked swiftly ahead of the male clerk who had been designated with the task of carrying the cumbersome parcels to her car. Opening the rear door on the driver's side, she stepped back to let him pass.

'Elizabeth.' A male voice spoke her name in warm surprise.

Turning, she saw Allan Marsden standing on the sidewalk in front of her car, a wide smile of pleasure directed at her. He was the administrator at the local city-county hospital and had been for the last year and a half. The townspeople were holding their breath to see how long he would stay. It was difficult to keep a man of Allan's caliber when they had to compete with larger cities that could offer him more prestigious jobs and better salaries. He was a young man, in his late thirties, which was young by their standards, and one they felt destined to go places.

'Hello, Allan.' Her greeting wasn't as warm as it usually was. Elizabeth was too anxious to be gone.

'I hadn't guessed that you would be in town over the lunch hour or I would have invited you to join me.' Sandy brown hair glistened a bronze shade, catching the sun when he inclined his head toward her with a rueful smile.

'I had a committee meeting and a few errands to run, so I was a bit pressed for time, anyway,' she assured him.

'That's all of them,' the young male clerk inserted

courteously as he closed the rear door of her car. 'Mr. Shaw wanted me to be sure to remind you that if any of the clothes didn't fit properly you were to bring them back.'

'Thank you,' Elizabeth nodded.

There was a puzzled light in Allan Marsden's eyes as he watched the clerk re-entering Shaw's Men's Shop. When his gaze swung curiously to Elizabeth, she very nearly didn't explain. But she liked Allan. She had accepted three dates with him, the last being nearly two weeks ago. He had been a pleasant, undemanding companion, although what she had told Jed was true, she didn't feel the need for a man's constant attention or companionship. With all those parcels in the back seat of the car bearing Shaw's name, it would be unfair to let Allan speculate why she should be buying men's clothes, especially considering that the news would be all over town within an hour that Jed was back.

'That was one of my more formidable tasks,' Elizabeth smiled, gesturing with her hand toward the rear of the car. 'My brother-in-law has just returned after a lengthy absence. His clothes haven't caught up with him yet, so I was appointed to buy him a few things.'

'Your brother-in-law?' His sandy brow lifted in surprise. 'Forgive me, I always assumed your late husband was an only child.'

'Jed is the younger brother, but he's been out of the country for several years.'

'Then you and Mrs. Carrel must be enjoying the reunion,' he smiled.

'Yes,' she agreed, knowing it was impossible to discuss the uneasy hostility that was tainting her life.

'I intended to call you tonight.' Allan stepped down from the curb, bringing himself closer to her. 'I purchased two tickets to your charity dinner and I was hoping that you would give me the privilege of being your escort.'

There was no reason for her not to accept, but Elizabeth found herself refusing. 'I'm sorry, Allan, but I do have to be there early to supervise the arrangements. As one of the committee chairmen, I'll have other duties throughout the evening that I'll have to see to. Perhaps it would be best if we simply planned to see each other there,' she suggested.

She sensed his objection to her alternate proposal, but he didn't express it or allow any disappointment to show. If he was interested in her and she was fairly certain of that, he seemed to have no intentions of rushing her. Perhaps it was because he didn't want to risk offending a Carrel and take the chance of having a black mark placed on his record by the family's influence in the community. That was a bitterly distasteful thought.

'The weatherman promises that Sunday is supposed to be a beautiful day. How about you and me and Amy going for a picnic? Say around two?' Allan countered.

Hesitating for a second, Elizabeth was unwilling to refuse a second invitation from him even though she was just as reluctant to accept it.

'Would you call me this evening, Allan?' she stalled.

'I'm not certain what plans Rebecca — my mother-in-law — might have made, with Jed back and all.'

'Of course I'll phone,' he smiled, 'and keep my fingers crossed.'

'I'll wait for your call,' Elizabeth promised, reaching for the handle of the driver's door. 'I really must get back now.'

'Yes, I'm due at the office, too. I'll talk to you this evening, Elizabeth.'

He was still standing on the sidewalk as she backed out of the parking place. She waved to him self-consciously, wishing she had refused the second invitation outright and wondering why she didn't want to go.

The Carrel home was two miles outside town, established many years ago by one of the ancestors who had combined his career as a judge with that of a gentleman farmer. In later years, the slight isolation from the rest of the community added to the image that they were apart from others like feudal lords of old.

Elizabeth didn't drive the car into the garage, but parked it next to the sidewalk to make it easier to unload and carry in the various packages. Amy was on the far side of the lawn under a large shade tree playing with her dolls. She waved, but didn't come over to greet her mother.

Balancing the precarious stack of packages in her arms, Elizabeth opened the front door of the house and walked in. Out of the corner of her eye, she spied her mother-in-law in the living room talking on the telephone. A pad was on the table beside her and a pencil in her hand. Rebecca glanced up and quickly, and vainly, removed the reading glasses from her nose.

Placing her hand over the receiver, she asked, 'Did you get everything on the list?'

'Yes,' Elizabeth nodded.

'You'd better take them right upstairs and hang them up before they get creased and need pressing,' Rebecca instructed. Once the order was given, she resumed her conversation with the person on the telephone.

It was tricky negotiating the stairs when the packages didn't enable her to see her feet, but Elizabeth made it to the top without incident. Walking to the end of the hallway, she found the door to Jed's bedroom ajar and she pushed it open. She paused on the threshold, reluctant to step inside.

There had always been an impersonal air that had made it just another bedroom. Now, there was something strangely different about it. Glancing about, the only thing she saw in the room that belonged to Jed was the duffle bag sitting in one corner. The bed was expertly made without a wrinkle. Considering the washed dishes in the sink, Elizabeth was certain the hand that had made it belonged to Jed and not her mother-in-law.

Entering the room, she spread the packages on the bed. Curiosity turned away from them, directing her footsteps to the adjoining bathroom. There she found neat evidence of Jed's habitation with razor, toothbrush, comb, and aftershave lotion sitting on the counter next to the wash basin, unmistakably male.

The heady fragrance of the cologned lotion touched her nose. Elizabeth decided it was this faint masculine scent that she had detected when she had entered the bedroom. With a guilty start, she realized that she was snooping and backtracked swiftly.

The trembling of her fingers surprised her as she began untying the packages and removing the clothes from the folds of the protective tissue. There was a strange curling sensation in the pit of her stomach and a faintly embarrassed warmth in her face. It was silly, she scolded herself. She had hung up men's clothes before. Why was she self-conscious about it now, she asked herself as she straightened a suit on its hanger.

Turning to walk to the closet, Elizabeth found herself staring into Jed's lean face. He was leaning against the door jamb in much the same lazy, slouching position as she had seen him yesterday, his hands stuffed in his pockets. The expression on his leanly carved face was unreadable, but there was faint amusement in the topaz-brown eyes that were studying her intently.

Her fingers closed nervously over the sleeve of the suit jacket as his gaze swept from her to the packages on the bed and back. With a poise she didn't feel, Elizabeth turned away and walked to the closet, trying to make the movement appear natural.

'Your mother thought you needed some additions to your wardrobe,' she explained off-handedly.

CHAPTER FOUR

'No doubt she discovered that when she went through my things last night.' His footsteps made no sound on the carpet, but Elizabeth could tell by the direction of his voice that he had moved to the bed. 'You have excellent taste, Liza. I should have you pick out my clothes all the time.'

'How did you know —' She spun around in surprise.

'That it was you?' Jed finished the question for her, plainly showing amusement in his expression now. 'I couldn't imagine Mother running the town's gauntlet when she could send you in her place.'

It had occurred to Elizabeth too that she had been used as a buffer for the town's curiosity, but she wasn't about to agree with Jed. She hung the suit in the closet and carried another wire hanger back to the bed.

'I opened our old account with Shaw's,' she told him. 'If there's anything I've overlooked, you can get it there.'

'I'm certain Mother's list was as thorough as her search,' Jed responded dryly.

'What makes you so certain that I wasn't the one who went through your things?' Elizabeth asked, driven by a surprising impulse to defend Rebecca.

'I guess there's just something about you that makes it difficult for me to visualize you pawing through a man's personal clothing,' he answered.

Bending over the jacket lying on the bed, she made a pretence of straightening the lapel to conceal the color that had swept into her cheeks.

'You did have your lunch, didn't you?' she asked in an effort to direct the conversation away from herself.

'Yes, at the Reisners.'

'You were gone so early this morning that I thought you might have gone there.' Elizabeth kept moving, occupying her hands with the clothes and walking back and forth to the closet to avoid any more than a brief, glance at Jed.

'Freda, Kurt's sister, seems to like you,' Jed commented idly. 'As she puts it, you're not a snob like my mother.'

'I like Freda too. She's very nice.'

'It's strange that with you two living so close, you don't see each other that much. Freda said that mostly you just bump into each other in town.'

'Well, you know how it is.' She gave a stiff, smiling shrug. 'I'm usually busy with a meeting of one kind or another. The free time that I do have, I like to spend with Amy.'

'That's commendable, but I'm sure Freda wouldn't object if you brought Amy along. She seems fond of children. As a matter of fact,' he continued with a complacent smile, 'I was invited to dinner on Sunday and Fred asked me to extend the invitation to you and your daughter. I'm to let her know if you're going.'

'That's impossible,' Elizabeth refused immediately.

'Why?' For all its softness, there was a knife-sharp thrust to his question.

'Because I've already made other plans,' she answered, suddenly glad that she hadn't refused Allan's invitation. It was a perfect excuse to avoid Jed's company.

'Really?' he mocked.

'Yes, really.' Irritation flashed in her green eyes that he should doubt she was speaking the truth. 'Amy and I have been invited to go on a picnic this Sunday.'

'Since you have a prior invitation, I'll give your apologies to Freda,' mocking skepticism was still in his tone.

'I am not making it up!' Elizabeth defended angrily. 'Allan Marsden did ask us out this Sunday. As a matter of fact, he's phoning tonight to confirm it. I thought your mother might plan something extra for your first Sunday home or I would have accepted immediately.' It was a small white lie, but one that she thought was justified under the circumstances. 'Since you aren't going to be home, there isn't any reason not to accept.'

'Allan Marsden?' Jed repeated. 'He must be new in town.'

· 'He's the hospital administrator.'

'Did the hospital ever raise the funds for that new clinic they were wanting?' he asked.

'No.' Suspicion loomed suddenly. 'Why?' she frowned.

'Curiosity, I suppose,' Jed shrugged disinterestedly, 'You mentioned the hospital and I wondered if they'd ever accomplished that proposed expansion.'

'If you're implying,' Elizabeth didn't believe his question had been prompted by casual curiosity, 'that Allan is seeing me in the hopes that, through me, your mother would be persuaded to make a sizeable donation, then you're wrong.'

'I'm sure I am,' he agreed smoothly.

'Allan leaves all that to his fund-raising committee.'

'Of course.'

Her lips tightened mutinously, the faint smile of mockery around his hard mouth goading her into losing her temper. His complacent tawny gold gaze studied the flashing fire of her green eyes.

'I doubt if Allan will even mention the hospital while we're on the picnic,' Elizabeth defended again, her fingers tugging impatiently at the suit jacket on the hanger.

'He wouldn't be much of a man if he did,' Jed stated with a curling suggestive smile. 'A warm summer afternoon, a shady glade, a blanket on the ground, and you as a companion on that blanket — I certainly wouldn't be thinking about my work.'

'You are impossible, Jed Carrel!' Elizabeth muttered. Walking angrily to the closet, she jammed the hanger hook on to the horizontal pole. 'You twist everything until it manages to come out cheap and sordid.'

'Do I do that?' He tipped his head to one side in laughing inquiry.

'You know very well you do.' She removed the tissue from the last box.

'I'd better offer my apologies, then.'

'Don't bother to pretend that you feel regret,' she cut in sharply. The last outfit was in the closet and she began busily gathering the boxes and tissues together, loading her arms with them. 'Now, if you'll excuse me, I have a great deal of work to do,' she flashed with biting sarcasm.

'Please accept my thanks for choosing my wardrobe, even if it was at Mother's instigation.' Again there was an underlying hint of mockery in his tone.

'It's only sheep's clothing, Jed,' Elizabeth tossed over her shoulder before leaving the room. His throaty laughter followed her down the hall.

The evening meal was routinely eaten at seven o'clock, a time that had been chosen not because Rebecca thought it fashionable, but because her late husband had always worked past the five o'clock office hours. The habit of eating at that hour had been too deeply ingrained to be changed after his death. Elizabeth had never minded it. It seemed to make the long evenings go by faster.

Allan Marsden telephoned her as he had promised, but his call came just as she was setting dinner on the table. She was on the living room extension when Jed wandered into the room. Staring at the brown suit he was wearing, one that she had chosen, she was stunned by the way it enhanced his dark virility. The suit fitted his muscular leannes so perfectly that it might have been tailor-made for him.

For a full second Elizabeth was aware only of his disturbing presence. Then she realized that Allan's voice was repeating the time of their planned outing and waiting for her acknowledgment. Forcing her clamoring senses to ignore Jed, she concentrated on the male voice on the telephone.

'Sunday at two is fine, Allan,' she agreed with false enthusiasm. 'Amy and I will be ready then. Are you certain there's nothing I can bring?'

'I've arranged for everything,' he replied. 'I didn't allow myself to consider the possibility that you might refuse. I'm glad you didn't, Elizabeth.'

'Yes, well,' she glanced apprehensively at Jed, realizing suddenly that he had no intention of leaving the room and that he was perfectly aware she was talking to Allan. He was deliberately eavesdropping. Anger flashed in her green eyes, prompting a flicker of amusement in the tawny eyes lazily watching her. 'I really have to let you go now, Allan. We were just sitting down to dinner.'

'Of course.' Allan didn't seem perturbed by her sudden desire to end the conversation. 'I'll see you Sunday.'

'Yes, Sunday,' she agreed quickly. 'Goodbye, Allan.'

She was already replacing the receiver as Allan's goodbye echoed into the room. There was an instant's hesitation as she considered commenting on Jed's bad manners at listening in before deciding such a comment would only lead to an arrogantly mocking reply.

'Dinner will be on the table in a few minutes,'

Elizabeth stated, turning away from him as she spoke.

'There's no need to hurry on my account,' Jed responded calmly.

Clamping her mouth shut, she refused to be baited into replying and walked swiftly from the room. He might not have felt the need for haste, but Elizabeth did. She wanted to get the meal over with as quickly as possible. A little voice told her that she was becoming much too conscious of him and she would be very foolish if she let him disturb the even tenor of her life.

In the middle of the meal, Elizabeth remembered that she hadn't told Rebecca of Allan Marsden's invitation. She disliked bringing it up in front of Jed, but she knew her mother-in-law had a church meeting that evening and would be leaving directly after dinner.

'Amy and I will be out this Sunday afternoon, Rebecca,' she said with false casualness. 'We've been invited —'

'Oh, are we going to the farm with Uncle Jed?' Amy burst in excitedly.

'What farm is this?' Rebecca demanded, her dark eyes centering immediately on Elizabeth, her interest not nearly as vague as it was a moment ago.

Darting a poisonous look at Jed, who appeared immune to its sting, she replied firmly, 'We aren't going to a farm. Amy and I have been invited on a picnic by Allan Marsden on Sunday.'

Amy frowned across the table, disappointment starting to cloud her face. 'Aren't we going to the farm?'

If it hadn't been for the distinct impression that Jed was deriving some sort of amused satisfaction from all this, Elizabeth's response would have been gentler.

'I just told you, Amy, that we're going for a picnic with Mr. Marsden.'

'What is all this nonsense about a farm?' Rebecca inserted, looking pointedly at her son.

'I've been invited to have Sunday dinner with the Reisners.' He nonchalantly buttered a hot crescent roll. 'Kurt suggested that perhaps Elizabeth might like to join us and bring Amy, but of course, she had a previous invitation from Mr. Marsden and had to decline.'

'I see,' was his mother's clipped response.

'But I wanted to go to the farm,' Amy declared with a defiantly pleading look.

'Well, I'm sorry, but we're going on the picnic.' Even as she spoke, Elizabeth knew she was being insensitively cold to her daughter. She should be quietly explaining that they could go to the farm another time instead of making a coldly worded order. It was Jed's fault.

'I don't want to go on your stupid old picnic!' The silverware in her daughter's hand was discarded angrily on to her plate, clanging loudly in accompaniment to her mutinous expression. 'I want to go to the farm and see the animals. I don't want to go with you!'

'That will be enough, Amy,' Elizabeth warned with firm softness.

'Maybe you can go another time,' Jed inserted, a

warm persuasive smile turning up the corners of his mouth.

'I never get to do what I want.' Her lower lip jutted out in a self-pitying pout, as Amy flashed a resentful glance at Elizabeth. 'I always have to do what *she* wants!'

Elizabeth was angered that Jed should attempt to quiet her daughter's temper. If he had not mentioned the invitation to the farm to Amy in the first place, none of this arguing would have occurred. Wrongly she directed this anger at Amy instead of the man at her right who deserved it.

'You will stop this sarcasm at once, Amy,' she ordered.

'I don't want to go on that picnic!' Tears began filling the brown eyes of her daughter.

'I think you'd better go to your room, Amy,' Elizabeth tried to speak calmly and control her own growing temper. 'When you can behave correctly at the table, you may return.'

'No, I will not go to my room!' The stiffly held back tears made Amy's voice tremble.

Although Jed might have been the instigator of the quarrel, Elizabeth recognized that she had handled it very badly. Sending Amy to her room was probably unfair punishment, but the open rebellion of her daughter at the order made it imperative that she carry it out, regardless of the knife of remorse that stabbed her heart.

Flashing Jed a speaking glance, Elizabeth rose from her chair and walked round to the opposite side of the table where Amy sat. With a downcast chin, Amy pushed her own chair away from the table. A tear slid down a round cheek as Amy refused to look at her mother, letting her sense of injustice be known.

'Come along, Amy,' Elizabeth said quietly. She touched the girl's shoulder with her hand and immediately Amy pulled away to walk rigidly toward the hall.

As Elizabeth turned to follow, she looked fully into Jed's bland expression. 'It's not her fault, Liza,' he said.

'I'm perfectly aware of that,' she snapped. 'You had no right to even mention the invitation to the farm without consulting me first. If anyone's to blame, it's you!'

Her long legs moved to follow her daughter's dragging steps. Once she was free of Jed's presence, she would explain to Amy why they were going on the picnic instead of to the farm. She would do so with the patience and understanding she should have exhibited in the first place. Yet there was the nagging memory that she had seized on Allan's invitation in order to have a plausible reason for refusing Jed's.

The large, patterned area rug cushioned the sound of the chair being pushed from the table. Not until a hand grabbed hold of Elizabeth's wrist to halt her forward movement did she realize that Jed had followed her. Her hair swirled about her face in an ebony cascade of curls as her head swung around to face him. His eyes had narrowed on to her expression of astonished outrage before they flickered briefly to

Amy, who had paused to listen near the stairwell.

'Go on up to your room, Amy,' Jed said firmly, but without anger or an ordering tone. 'I want to have a little discussion with your mother.'

Amy hesitated, then the stairway door opened and closed. Next there was the sound of her footsteps slowly carrying her up the stairs.

'I don't see that we have anything to discuss,' Elizabeth said tautly, tossing her head back to glare into his lean, carved features.

'But I do,' he answered in the same firm voice that he had used with Amy.

'Perhaps we do,' she agreed suddenly with a haughty lift of her chin. She didn't attempt to pull free of his hand. The iron grip of his fingers already told her it would be useless. 'I'd like to hear your explanation. After I'd already turned down the invitation I think you were terribly cruel to mention it to Amy and try to use her to persuade me to change my mind.'

'In the first place, I didn't tell Amy about the invitation,' Jed answered curtly.

'Do you expect me to believe that?' Elizabeth demanded. 'I hadn't even mentioned to her that we were going on the picnic Sunday, let alone tell her that we'd turned down your invitation. There's no one else who could have told her about it, except you!'

His mouth thinned dangerously narrow. 'The only conversation I had with your daughter concerned my whereabouts this morning. I *did* tell her I'd been at the Reisners' farm.'

'And that you were invited on Sunday and so were we,' she inserted.

'I did tell her that I was going there on Sunday,' he admitted tightly, 'but I didn't mention that you were invited. Or that you'd made other plans for the day.'

'Then where did she get the idea that we might visit the farm?' Elizabeth asked with cold disbelief.

'As I recall,' amber lights were flashing warning signals in his eyes, 'Amy asked if she might go over some time to see the puppies I had told her about. I said she would have to ask you.'

'That's a likely story,' she scoffed contemptuously. 'Why can't you admit that you were trying to prejudice her into influencing me?'

'Because I don't care whether you ever go to the Reisners' or not,' Jed snapped. 'I merely extended Kurt's invitation. If I wanted you to change your mind — there are other means of accomplishing it without involving a child.'

'Then why did you bring the farm up with Amy at all?' Elizabeth continued to protest angrily. 'Were you jealous of the fact that we have a warm relationship? Did you want to make it as miserable and bitter as the one between you and your mother?'

'I don't give a damn what you think!' He released her wrist abruptly, glowering fury in his face. 'If you want to paint me black, then go ahead! The only opinion that matters to me is my own.'

In the next second he was striding away and Elizabeth was staring after him in open-mouthed and angry amazement. He disappeared into the front

72

hallway. Then the front door slammed with resounding violence.

'Elizabeth!' Rebecca Carrel's voice called to her imperiously from the dining room. 'Was that Jed who just stormed out of the door?'

'Yes,' she acknowledged, her voice trembling in indignation that he should have walked out on her like that.

'You might as well come back in here and finish your meal,' her mother-in-law ordered.

Elizabeth glanced to the dining room archway, then toward the stairway and the room at the top where Amy was waiting. She forced herself to swallow back the tight knot of anger.

'In a moment, Rebecca,' she said in a more controlled tone. 'I want to have a talk with Amy first.'

'I think it would be best if you left her alone for a while. It will give her an opportunity to consider how unforgivably rude and cheeky she was. An apology is definitely in order after her ill-mannered behavior at the table.' There was a light pause before Rebecca added in a bitter tone, 'I don't see why she doesn't take after her father.'

Instead of Jed her uncle, Elizabeth finished for the older woman. Yes, Amy's aggressively independent nature was more indicative of Jed than Jeremy. Amy was never satisfied that things were to be done in a certain way because that was proper or expected.

Breathing in deeply, she walked toward the steps. In the back of her mind, she knew that when she had explained to Amy why they were going on the picnic, she

73

was going to find out exactly what Jed had told her about the farm. She couldn't believe that her daughter might think they would go to the farm only on the strength of what Jed had indicated that he had told her. As soon as Amy had given her the proof she needed, she intended to confront Jed with it.

The outcome of her discussion with Amy did not produce the satisfying results that Elizabeth had anticipated. She had been forced to accept the fact that Jed had told the truth. It had been Amy's imagination that made her leap to the conclusion that they were going to the farm. It was a fairly logical deduction, Elizabeth had decided silently, since it was the farm that was uppermost in Amy's mind.

As for the picnic, her daughter's lack of enthusiasm at the prospect didn't improve after their talk. She had grudgingly agreed to go, but had refused to return to the dinner table. The sulky droop to her mouth had remained despite Elizabeth's lighthearted cajoling, a portent of things to come.

Amy's boredom on the picnic couldn't have been expressed more plainly if she had spent the entire afternoon sitting on the blanket and yawning. Elizabeth had been too self-conscious and irritated by her rudeness to react naturally. The responses she made to Allan's attempts to lighten the atmosphere were stilted and false, increasing the discomfort that saturated each moment of the outing. Her embarrassment had increased when Allan had suggested they call it a day at four o'clock, a scant two hours since it had begun.

To make matters worse, Amy had mumbled an

ungracious 'thank you' and bolted from the car the minute Allan stopped it in front of their house. Elizabeth had stared after her for a full minute before turning to Allan, the wryly twisting line of his mouth marking his expression.

'I must apologize for my daughter,' she murmured self-consciously. 'Her behavior today was unforgivable. She really isn't usually this sulky and —'

'You don't need to explain,' Allan smiled understandingly, taking one of the hands that were twisted together in her lap and holding it in his own. 'Children tend to be a bit selfish about their parents, especially if they have only one.'

'It wasn't jealousy.' Elizabeth shifted uncomfortably. 'I took my anger with someone else out on her the other day, and she hasn't forgiven me for it.'

'I can't imagine you being angry. You're much too beautiful.' The smooth compliment sprang easily from his lips.

'I am human,' she smiled nervously to shrug it aside.

'That's encouraging.' His gaze swept over her windtouseled hair, curling jet black against her lightly tanned skin, then it returned to the jade greenness of her eyes. Leaning forward, Allan pressed a warm, lingering kiss against the roundness of her lips. 'I'll see you at the dinner if not before.'

When he straightened away from her, Elizabeth reached for the door handle, then paused with the door partially ajar. 'Thank you, Allan, for — for everything,' she offered in gratitude for his understanding.

'Maybe another time the three of us can make it a more enjoyable day,' he suggested.

'Yes, another time,' she agreed uncertainly, andd stepped from the car.

Waving once as he reversed out of the drive, Elizabeth walked toward the house. Amy's behavior should not be allowed to go by without comment, but she was reluctant to lecture her about it. Sighing heavily, she opened the front door.

The sound of Amy's laughter halted her on the threshold. The entire afternoon she had barely smiled at all, now she was laughing. Elizabeth's chin lifted at the sight of her daughter standing in front of the bending form of Jed. His tawny gaze saw her first, a watchfulness in his expression despite the wide grin on his face. Then Amy glanced over her shoulder and the smile faded from her mouth. Apology flickered in her dark eyes before she dashed toward the stairs.

Jed stood upright as Elizabeth shut the door behind her. A flashfire of irritation raced through her veins, angered that he had prompted Amy's laughter when Allan had tried so hard and failed.

'I didn't expect you back so soon,' Jed commented.

'That makes two of us, because neither did I,' she retorted coldly.

'What happened?'

There was a chilling arch to her brow. 'Didn't Amy tell you? Her little sulk succeeded in making the picnic totally miserable for everyone.'

'No, she didn't mention it,' he returned evenly.

'Really? I was certain that's what the two of you were laughing about,' she said in a faintly accusing tone. It completely slipped her mind that she still had not apologized for doubting his word the other night. She had not had the opportunity to speak to him alone and she had no intention of apologizing to him in front of Rebecca or Amy.

'I wouldn't worry.' Jed tipped his head to the side as he mockingly inspected her. 'I doubt if your boyfriend will be put off by one less than satisfying afternoon.'

'He's not —' Elizabeth checked the denial that Allan was her boyfriend. It would only earn her another taunt. 'As a matter of fact,' she said coolly, 'I'll be seeing Allan at the charity dinner next Saturday night.'

'I hope you didn't agree to let him escort you there,' he observed dryly.

'What business of yours would it be if I did?' she challenged.

'It would be Mother's business, not mine,' Jed corrected. There was an indication of some secret knowledge in the wryly amused curl of his mouth.

'Rebecca doesn't dictate my social life,' Elizabeth stated firmly.

'That's one you can argue out with her.' Uninterest moved across his face as he turned away.

'What makes you think that I would need to argue with her?' she demanded, drawing an over-the-shoulder glance from Jed.

In the fleeting instant, there was the look of a rogue about him, youthful and daring. His eyes glittered with mischievous satisfaction, totally erasing the cynicism that was nearly always present in one form or another. But more, the hard look was gone, the look of a man who had seen much that was unpleasant.

'Mother has decided that I'm to make my public debut at your dinner next week,' Jed replied. 'She intends the Carrel family to attend this social function as a unit.'

'And you're going?' she murmured doubtfully.

'You've forgotten, Liza.' His gaze narrowed slightly. 'I came back to make some sort of peace. That requires compromise. So yes, I am attending your black tie banquet.'

CHAPTER FIVE

'JED has arrived with the sitter, Elizabeth. Are you ready yet?' Rebecca called.

Halting the tube of coral lipstick inches from her mouth, Elizabeth answered, 'In a minute!'

'Well, please hurry,' her mother-in-law returned impatiently. 'I don't want to be the first to arrive, but neither do I want to be the last.'

Sighing ruefully, Elizabeth looked into the mirror, wishing for the umpteenth time that she hadn't allowed Rebecca to persuade her to arrive at the dinner with Rebecca and Jed. She had thought she had the perfect excuse, the supervision of the pre-dinner arrangements. But Rebecca had adamantly insisted that as chairman, Elizabeth should appoint someone else to the task. Now she realized that she had given in because of the subconscious re-echoing of Jed's words concerning compromise and making peace. So she had compromised her own judgment by agreeing to Rebecca's demands.

The silk underlining of her white lace dress rustled as she walked toward the hallway door. Turning the doorknob, she remembered her matching shawl and evening bag were lying on the bed. She retrieved them quickly from the blue satin coverlet. Her pulse was behaving erratically and her nerves were so jittery that she was certain she hadn't been this disturbed by her first date. But her outward composure revealed none of her inner agitation.

Amy was waiting for her at the bottom of the stairs. Her brown eyes widened and her mouth rounded into a sighing, complimentary 'Oh!' A smile of genuine pleasure eased the tense muscles around Elizabeth's mouth.

'Do I look all right?' She turned slowly for her daughter's benefit.

'Oh yes, Mom, you look scrumptious!' Amy assured her in a breathy voice.

'Hello, Cindy,' Elizabeth greeted the schoolgirl standing in the hall.

'Hello, Mrs. Carrel. That's a lovely gown.' The young girl gazed almost enviously at the gently moulding long lace gown. There was a telltale glimmer of braces as she barely moved her lips to speak. Elizabeth remembered her own schoolgirl dreams of enchantment whenever she had seen adults dressed in formal attire and smiled.

'Thank you,' she nodded, wishing she could cast aside her misgivings toward the evening and catch some of the stardust that was in Cindy's eyes. 'Did my mother-in-law give you the telephone number where we can be reached if you have any problems?'

'Yes, she did, but I'm sure everything will be all right,' the girl added hastily.

'Elizabeth, Jed is waiting in the car,' Rebecca stepped into the archway of the front hallway.

Bending to kiss her daughter's cheek, Elizabeth teased, 'Be good for a change, Amy.'

Brown eyes twinkled back at her. 'I'll try,' she said as she wrinkled her nose impishly.

Following her mother-in-law to the car, Elizabeth took her place in the back seat, murmuring a polite thanks when Jed held the door open for her. The country club and adjoining golf course was only a mile or so from th e which made the journey short. But Elizabeth was conscious of Jed's faint air of preoccupation. She was almost certain his silence couldn't be blamed on the evening before them.

Silently she acknowledged that his dark evening clothes suited him. It wasn't until they had arrived at the club that she noticed it was not the suit she had picked out for him. The entrance lights fully illuminated the expertly tailored suit as he opened the car door for her, offering a hand out. Elizabeth frowned her bewilderment. The material of his suit and the white silk shirt were much more expensive than any she had seen locally.

'What's the matter?' One corner of his mouth lifted as he tossed the car keys to the parking attendant. He touched the dark lapel with his finger. 'Don't you like the suit?'

'Yes,' she answered quickly, avoiding the roguish light glittering in his eyes. She made a pretense of adjusting her rectangular shawl. 'It's just that you didn't mention that you'd bought anything when you went to Cleveland last week.'

'I wasn't aware that I needed to,' he replied, lightly

touching her elbow to guide her around the car to where Rebecca waited.

Pressing her lips tightly together, Elizabeth didn't comment. Jed had been absent most of the week, a situation that had preyed on her nerves since she had never been entirely certain when he might turn up. His explanations, even to his mother, as to where he had been were vague and uninformative. Elizabeth couldn't make up her mind whether his mysteriousness was deliberate or merely an extension of his personality.

When they reached Rebecca's side, she preceded them into the club, her head tilted regally as though she were leading a royal procession. In answer, heads turned at their approach. Curiosity was the main reaction, cloaked in the guise of greeting. The farther they walked into the small reception area where cocktails were being served, the more conscious Elizabeth became of another reaction.

Her gaze slid sideways to the man at her side. Six foot, lean, with thick, carelessly waving tobacco brown hair and rakishly carved features, Jed Carrel was a compellingly attractive man. He was not the handsomest or the tallest man in the room. And Elizabeth realized that he was not holding everyone's attention simply because he was a Carrel or because he was a Carrel who had become an outcast by his family.

Perhaps a part of it was the worldly look in his eyes, that intimation that he had seen and experienced much without ever revealing what had happened. But more, Elizabeth knew, with a certainty that it was the potent virility, his maleness that silently challenged women.

She was still making a surreptitious study of him when Jed turned his head and held her gaze. In that charged second she knew that he had been aware of her inspection all along. It was there in the laughing glitter of his eyes.

'What do you suppose they're thinking?' he murmured to her in an aside as he nodded and greeted the various people who were acknowledging them.

Elizabeth gave a quick hello to Mr. Shaw and his wife before answering Jed's question in a voice as soft as his. 'That you've grown into a fine-looking man.' The smile she gave him as she looked into his face was cool and controlled. 'No doubt the mothers are wondering if they should let their daughters near you and —' pausing for emphasis, 'whether they're too old to catch you themselves.'

His quiet chuckle touched only her ears. 'I didn't expect cynicism from you, Liza.'

The captivation in his smile caught her by surprise. She hadn't realized he could be so charming if he chose. She quickly averted her gaze, feeling the warmth rising in her neck, but bringing only an attractive pink tint to her cheeks.

'I didn't mean it to sound cynical,' she replied.

At that moment Barbara Hopkins detached herself from a younger group of adults and glided forward to meet Elizabeth. Her friend's eyes kept straying to Jed, leaving Elizabeth in little doubt as to whom she was really interested in meeting. It was only natural, she supposed. After all, Jed could be classified as an eligible bachelor and there wasn't an abundance of unattached males in Carrelville.

'Elizabeth!' Barbara called gaily, reaching out with a ringed hand in greeting. 'That's a stunning gown.'

Patiently Elizabeth returned the greeting and compliment, before introducing Jed. Barbara's coy gaze vaguely irritated Elizabeth when it was directed at Jed, but he didn't seem to find it too sweet.

'So you are Elizabeth's tennis friend?' he smiled, holding Barbara's hand longer than Elizabeth thought was necessary.

'Oh, yes, we play at least once a week. Do you play, Mr. Carrel?'

'Jed, please,' he corrected smoothly with a brief inquiring tilt of his head, 'if I may call you Barbara?' His answer was a wide, satisfied smile of agreement. 'I do play tennis, although not recently.'

'Perhaps we can arrange a game of doubles.' Barbara glanced pointedly at Elizabeth, letting her know it wasn't an idle suggestion. 'You'll have to persuade Allan to be your partner.'

The reference to Allan Marsden made Elizabeth conscious of the man standing to her left. At the mention of his name, he stepped forward, handing Elizabeth one of the drinks he held in his hand.

'Hello, Elizabeth. I've been waiting for you to come.' He smiled pleasantly as he spoke, a vague questioning light in his eyes.

Not meeting his gaze squarely, she replied, 'there was a last-minute adjustment of the schedules,' completely aware that she had put him off escorting her

84

tonight because she was supposed to be here early.

Jed's hand shifted from her elbow to the back of her waist as he leaned around her, a faint intimacy in his touch that she found unnerving. 'You must be Allan Marsden. Elizabeth has mentioned you.' He extended his hand. 'I'm Jed Carrel.'

'Welcome home,' Allan said, shaking the hand firmly and smiling. 'I imagine that's been said to you many times.'

Tawny eyes slid to Elizabeth, mocking her quickly ricocheting look. 'Not all that many times that I've grown tired of hearing it,' Jed responded.

Her fingers tightened around the cocktail glass Allan had given her as she wondered if anyone had told Jed that before. Certainly she hadn't, and neither had his mother. It would be ironic if his first words of welcome were given by a stranger. Ironic and cruel.

'I see you've been here long enough to locate the cocktail bar,' Jed observed, glancing to the iced drink in Allan's hand.

'Let me show you where it is,' Barbara offered quickly.

Her friend was wasting no time in staking a claim on Jed, Elizabeth thought with a flash of bitterness that surprised her. Jed's gaze laughed openly at the darkening green of her eyes.

'You will excuse me, won't you, little sister?' The grooves around his mouth deepened with a suppressed smile.

'Of course,' she nodded. Her skin felt suddenly cool where his hand had warmed the back of her waist.

Some of the chill crept into her voice, tight and dull.

'He certainly isn't what I expected,' Allan commented quietly as he watched Jed being slowly led through the crowd by Barbara.

'Oh? Why not?' Elizabeth asked. Her attempt at vague interest came out frosty and defensive.

Allan glanced at her sharply, taking his time in wording his answer. 'From the rumors I've heard since his return, I suppose I expected someone more belligerent and arrogant. His self-assurance and easy charm caught me by surprise, I guess.'

'I suppose it would.' Elizabeth didn't want to discuss Jed, averting her gaze from his hypnotic form still discernible on the far side of the room.

'Was your husband like him?'

'They were very nearly total opposites,' she answered curtly. Then with an abrupt change of subject, she inserted, 'I want to apologize for the mixup this evening. I hope you didn't arrive too early thinking to find me here.'

'No, I didn't.' Allan followed her lead.

But it was impossible to completely avoid the topic of Jed. Nearly everyone she and Allan talked to had some comment or question about him. And her sensitive radar never lost track of where he was located in the room..No matter how casually she glanced around the room, her gaze invariably homed in on Jed. She couldn't avoid noticing that he had that ability to hold himself apart from others while appearing to join in with their laughter and conversation.

At the long dinner table, Elizabeth and Allan were

seated on the opposite side of the table from Jed and ever-constant Barbara. Fortunately they were several chairs down the table. Yet Elizabeth couldn't avoid seeing him whenever she glanced in that direction.

As the meal progressed, she found herself becoming sickened by her girlfriend's actions. The way Barbara kept leaning confidentially toward him and accidentally brushing against him robbed her appetite. The boldness of the flirtation left little to the imagination of the onlookers, and they were many. Jed did not rebuff Barbara's advances. In fact, Elizabeth was certain that the amused interest in his eyes was meant to encourage.

By the time the last course was served, anger was smouldering inside her, igniting into hot flames whenever her eyes wavered toward Jed, which was becoming increasingly often. The merry sound of Barbara's laughter drew her gaze again, and this time it was met and held by Jed's. As his mouth quirked in lazy amusement at one corner, Elizabeth realized her eyes were revealing her distaste and disgust for their conduct.

Then Barbara's hand was touching the sleeve of his suit jacket in light possession, drawing his attention back to her. Elizabeth stared at her untouched dessert plate, her nerves so taut that she felt at any moment they would snap. Smiling stiffly at Allan, she excused herself from the table. She cursed silently at the way she was drawing attention to herself, but she didn't care. She had to get away from the table to regain her perspective.

In the powder room, she waved aside the administrations of the attendant, taking deep, calming breaths and willing herself to relax the tense cords in her neck. Turning on the cold water tap, she let the chilling liquid stream over the insides of her wrists to cool the feverish heat in her veins.

When she left the powder room, Elizabeth still didn't feel sufficiently in control to return to the table. Luckily her role as chairman of the dinner committee allowed her to enter the kitchens without a questioning look as to her motives. She deliberately took her time waiting until the moment when the guests were leaving the dining area to return to the reception room where a small dance band had been engaged to play.

Unfortunately Allan was standing with Jed and Barbara. Elizabeth hesitated for an instant, about to change direction, when Jed saw her. Fixing a smile on her face, she tried to pretend that she had just that moment seen them, but she didn't think Jed was fooled.

'Is everything in order?' Allan inquired with a welcoming smile.

'It seems to be,' she answered in what she hoped sounded like a satisfied sigh.

'I'm glad my only responsibility was in selling tickets,' said Barbara, her hand resting on the inside of Jed's arm. 'Now I can simply enjoy the party.'

'How astute of Elizabeth to select you to sell tickets,' Jed murmured, glancing at the blonde. 'I doubt that there was a man in town who refused to buy one from you, unless his wife was around.'

'Jed Carrel!' Barbara sounded properly shocked, but it was only a pose.

Elizabeth moistened her lips and turned to Allan. 'I hear the band is very good,' she said.

As if on cue, the band struck the opening chord of the first song. A hand lightly touched her arm. Elizabeth stared at its owner, unable to keep the disdain from glittering viridescently in her eyes at Jed's touch.

'It's only fitting,' he said quietly, a mocking challenge in his gaze, 'that since a Carrel is mainly responsible for this evening, we should lead the first dance.'

If she hadn't been so certain that it was what Jed expected, she would have refused. Instead she inclined her head in agreement and allowed him to take her hand. She sensed that neither Allan nor Barbara approved, but there wasn't any way they could protest.

Two couples had started on to the empty dance floor at the band's prelude to 'Beautiful Ohio'. They stepped near the edge when they saw Jed leading Elizabeth on to the floor. In the center of the floor, he turned her into his arms and stopped. His eyes swept over her almost grimly unenthusiastic expression with a lazily relaxed study.

'I feel as if I'm holding a cold fish. Loosen up, Liza,' Jed chided softly. 'And smile. You're not going to an execution.'

'I'm not?' But she smiled sweetly, forcing her muscles to become pliant under his gliding touch as he led her into the first step.

The firm pressure of the hand at her back made it easy for her to follow his lead. With each step she became more fluid, the rigidity lessening as if answering the challenge of his natural grace. From the first he had held her gaze. Now Elizabeth found herself becoming fascinated by the darkening amber hues. They glided twice around the floor before the first couple joined them. Jed slowed their steps and confined their route to a smaller area of the floor.

'Isn't it better to have these duty dances over in the beginning?' The spell of the dreamy, sentimental tune was broken by his faintly sarcastic tone.

Breaking free of his compelling features, Elizabeth stared at the contrast of the white shirt collar against the dark tan of his throat. Her own throat felt dry and parched, caused no doubt by the heat that was emanating from the hand spread on her back and the rock-firm muscles of his thighs.

'Yes, much better,' Elizabeth agreed huskily, straining slightly against his arm so she wouldn't be held too closely against his hips.

'Now everyone is saying how very well we dance together.' From her side vision she could see that his eyes never left her face, although her own made a quick sweep of the room to affirm his statement. They were the object of much interested scrutiny. 'Had I not danced with you, they would have been wondering all night why.'

'Would you have cared?' she challenged.

Jed grinned. 'I wonder what the townspeople would say if they knew how easily sarcasm slips from the alluring mouth of the young and beautiful widow Carrel. That's what they call you, you know — the young widow Carrel.' The line of his firm mouth became crooked with derision. 'They regard you as a courageous figure, rising above the tragedy that befell you so young, always behaving with the utmost decorum, and faithful to the loving memory of your husband. Perhaps you should apply for sainthood?'

A betraying crimson flush raged across her face. 'Must you make it sound as if it's something I should be ashamed of?'

'Blushing — another rare commodity.' There was the sensation of an invisible shrug. 'I've always been skeptical of the "goody two-shoes" in the world, maybe because very early in life I became tired of being reminded what a good boy Jeremy was when I knew all along that he wasn't any different from me. I took the blame for some of his pranks too many times.'

'Must we discuss Jerry?' Elizabeth demanded uneasily. There was the sickening knowledge that she couldn't visualize her husband's face without the benefit of his picture.

'Is the memory too painful?' Jed taunted, his eyes narrowing on her averted profile.

Ebony dark curls touched the bareness of her back as she tilted her head to direct the flaring resentment in her green eyes up to his face. She longed to startle him with the admission that her recollection of those brief moments as Jeremy's wife was hazy, that she had almost forgotten he had ever existed until Jed returned. The memory of her first meeting with Jed was clearer and more vivid than her wedding night with her husband, his brother. She obeyed the inner caution that checked the admission.

'Think what you like,' she replied bitterly. 'You will anyway, regardless of what I say.'

'Do you know what I'm thinking?' he murmured with piercing softness. 'I'm curious why you're so defensive every time I mention his name.'

'Maybe it's because you are so offensive,' she retorted.

The song ended and she moved as swiftly as possible out of his arms. Her legs were treacherously unsteady. She realized that they had been all along, but the firmness of Jed's supporting hold had blinded her to it. His rangy stride had him at her side almost instantly, an arm circling the back of her waist as he guided her off the dance floor.

'Out of condition?' he mocked in an undertone.

'I believe it's the immense relief I feel that I don't have to dance with you again,' Elizabeth muttered savagely beneath her breath.

'Ah, there's your adoring Allan,' Jed smiled wickedly, 'waiting patiently for me to return you to him. Do you know, he reminds me of Jerry?'

'He doesn't look at all like him,' she answered sharply, secure in that statement since Alan was light-complected and Jeremy had been dark.

'Not in looks,' he chuckled, 'in temperament. Your Allan will never make waves. He'd be too concerned he'd upset the boat he was in.'

'What's the matter, Jed?' Her temper flared. 'Are you jealous because Allan has made a success of his life while you've come home a failure?'

'Oh, Liza!' Anger trembled in the sighing way Jed spoke her name despite the tight control in his voice. He breathed in deeply, caution lights flashing in his narrowed look. 'You make waves, too, don't you?'

Elizabeth almost ran the last few steps to Allan, intimidated more than she cared to admit by the anger she had provoked. There was the frightening knowledge that she had been making waves and the last one had nearly swamped her boat. Allan was the lifeline and she clung to his hand tightly.

Barbara had been waiting with Allan and she stepped forward quickly to meet Jed. He smiled at her as if in answer to the silent promise in her eyes. The same feeling of distaste began to tie Elizabeth's stomach into knots again.

'I'm in need of a drink, Barbara,' Jed stated, sliding a still smouldering look to Elizabeth. 'Why don't you lead me to the bar again?'

'Would you like a cocktail?' Allan offered.

Elizabeth felt in need of a burning jolt of alcohol, but not for anything did she want to follow Jed and Barbara. She refused firmly, the vigorous shake of her head trying to dispel the warning voices that kept whispering to her.

The evening had been hopelessly ruined, but she fought against it, determined to have as much fun as Jed. Allan was most attentive and her smiles and laughter encouraged him even more. It was unkind and unfair to focus her green eyes on him whenever Jed's shadow fell on her. No matter how hard she tried, Elizabeth was unable to ignore him.

Despite Barbara's attempt to monopolize him, Elizabeth noticed when he danced with others. More duty dances, she had thought viciously. Resentment seethed behind her smiles. It exploded into disgust and hatred every time she saw Jed and Barbara on the dance floor.

By midnight her head was pounding from the tension of constantly suppressing her emotions. She was certain she could not endure another minute without screaming. Her nerves were raw. Her stomach churned with nauseating constancy. She nearly cried with relief when she saw Rebecca approaching her.

'I think it's time we should leave, Elizabeth,' her mother-in-law stated after smiling politely to Allan. We promised the sitter we wouldn't be late.'

Inwardly Elizabeth recognized that Rebecca was not motivated by any consideration of the schoolgirl watching Amy. Just as her mother-in-law didn't like to be the first to arrive, she didn't like to be the last to leave. Besides, it wouldn't be proper for a Carrel to be too fond of parties.

The idea was forming in Allan's expression to offer to take Elizabeth home. She knew that once outside the walls of the club, she would not be pleasant company. Considering the way she had behaved toward him all evening, he would find her changed attitude puzzling and totally unlike her. Before he could speak, she did.

'I'm ready whenever you are, Rebecca,' she agreed quickly, dredging into her reserves to turn to Allan and smile. 'Perhaps we can get together for lunch one day this week.'

'Yes —' he hesitated slightly before resigning himself to her half promise. 'Yes, we'll do that.'

A brief exchange of goodbyes and Elizabeth and Rebecca were walking toward the exit. 'Did you get the keys from Jed?' Elizabeth inquired, clicking open her evening bag to see if by chance she had a spare set for the car.

'Jed is having the car brought around now,' Rebecca frowned. 'Where did you think he was?'

Elizabeth glanced back toward the group, surprised to see Barbara smiling and dancing with someone else. 'I supposed he was going to stay for a while,' she murmured.

'He is leaving with us,' was the firm response, as if any other action was unthinkable.

The car was at the door when they walked out, the parking attendant holding both side doors open. Jed was behind the wheel with the motor running. He didn't seem at all surprised that Elizabeth was returning with them and not with Allan. The instant the doors were closed, he put the car in gear and turned it down the lane.

'It's such a relief to be away from that noise,' Rebecca sighed. 'It does get on a person's nerves after a while.'

Elizabeth's throbbing temples echoed the sentiment, but she didn't place all the blame on the noisy gaiety of

the party. It had only been an irritant. In the con-
cealment of the darkness, she cast daggers at the
strong profile of the driver.

'I was talking to Clive Bennet tonight,' her mother-
in-law continued. 'He's one of the directors of the
country club. The position of club manager will be
vacant the first of September. I sounded him out on
the possibility of you taking it on, Jed. The club pretty
well runs itself. The golf pro manages the greens and
the restaurant manager sees to both the food and
drink. Yours would be a strictly supervisory role.'

'Thanks, Mother, but no, thanks,' Jed refused
evenly.

'What exactly is it that you intend to do?' Impatience sharpened Rebecca's voice to a cutting edge.

'What I've been doing.'

'Which is nothing,' she retorted.

He smiled thinly. 'I know you were motivated by the
best of intentions to make the inquiry on my behalf,
Mother, but I believe I can decide for myself what I
want.'

'I swear you'll be a wastrel the rest of your life,'
Rebecca muttered.

'But then it is my life, isn't it, Mother?' His gaze slid
to her briefly before returning to the highway
illuminated by the car's headlights.

He was so arrogantly certain that he knew what was
right, Elizabeth seethed. She saw him glance at her
reflection in the mirror and directed her gaze out the
side window. If only he would leave, she wished silently, and stop disrupting the quiet pattern of her life.

CHAPTER SIX

'DID Amy behave herself?' Elizabeth removed the required amount of money from her purse and handed it to the young girl.

'I didn't have any trouble at all,' Cindy assured her, stifling a yawn as she stuffed the money in her shoulder bag.

'I hope we didn't keep you too late,' Elizabeth smiled stiffly, brushing back a strand of black hair, aware of Jed watching them near the front door waiting to take the baby-sitter home. 'I wouldn't want your parents to be worried.'

'Oh, no, Mrs. Carrel, I'm sure they're not worried. I explained that you were going out to a dance tonight and they don't expect me back until much later.'

Nodding, Elizabeth turned to make the polite request of Jed that he take Cindy home, but he was already straightening away from the door, smiling at the schoolgirl self-consciously returning his look.

'If you aren't expected home right away, then that means we can take the long way home, doesn't it?' he winked.

It was an innocently teasing remark, but Elizabeth's fingers curled into her palm. A scarlet blush was enveloping the girl's face. Her own teenage years were not so far behind that Elizabeth didn't recognize the symptoms of a schoolgirl crush. At that age it didn't matter that the suggestion had been made in jest. What mattered was that Jed had noticed her at all.

It wasn't the first time that evening that Elizabeth had seen such a reaction. Women in their sixties had blossomed just as quickly under the attention of his charm. It seemed every female was vulnerable to his considerable masculine force. The knowledge irritated her, more so perhaps because there was a certain vulnerability within herself.

'Goodnight, Cindy.' There was a faintly clipped edge to her voice that arched Jed's brow in mockery.

'Goodnight, Mrs. Carrel,' Cindy returned, glancing swiftly at Jed through the tips of her lashes as he held the door open for her.

A tiny smile that bordered on the flirtatious turned up the corners of the girl's mouth as she started through the door. The smile wasn't wide enough to reveal the corrective braces on her teeth, and thus remind Jed of her immaturity. Elizabeth whirled away in anger before the door closed behind them.

The impetus of it carried her swiftly up the stairs to her room, but there was no relief in the solitude of the room. The screaming tautness of her nerves did not relax within the security of the four walls. If anything, the pain in her head throbbed more furiously than before. She paced the room restlessly for several minutes, wishing for a warm glass of milk to soothe her tension, but reluctant to go back downstairs to get it. Rebecca would be sure to hear her and come to find out what was wrong, and a conversation with her mother-in-law was the last thing Elizabeth wanted.

With impatient movements, she stripped off the lace evening gown. Tears of frustration filled her eyes when she poked a finger through her nylon pantyhose, ruining them beyond use. After slipping her pale green nightgown over her head, she donned the matching silk robe, securing the sash around her waist, and walked into the adjoining bathroom. Hurriedly she swallowed two aspirins, washing them down with a glassful of water and praying they would work quickly.

Her hands shook traitorously as she creamed the make-up from her face. Without the cosmetic mask, she lost her air of sophistication. There was a vaguely yearning light in her green eyes. It reminded Elizabeth of something. Then the answer flashed through her mind. It was the same wishful look that she had seen in Cindy's eyes. She slammed the jar of cleansing cream on to the shelf in disgust.

Swiftly she returned to the bedroom. Glancing at the small clock near her bed, she quickly worked out that Jed would have already left Cindy at her home and be en route to — where? Her lips compressed into a thin line. He would no doubt be returning to the country club and Barbara's waiting arms. Yes, she thought grimly, that was exactly what he would do. He had willingly left to bring her and Rebecca home so he wouldn't be encumbered with them later. He and Barbara would have the night free to — She left the thought uncompleted as a nauseating shudder trembled through her. She didn't want to think.

Her imagination was becoming too vivid. She needed to rid her mouth of its bitter taste. Forcing a silent fluidness into her legs, Elizabeth stepped into the hallway, quietly turned the doorknob to her daughter's room and walked in.

Standing beside the bed, she stared at the small sleeping figure, the dark hair against the white pillow appearing black in the dim light. The covers were half thrown off and Elizabeth pulled them back over her daughter. A serene joy filled her heart during moments like this, a contentment in knowing that, God willing, she would always be there to look after her daughter.

Sighing wistfully, she turned away from the bed. If only she had someone of her own to look after her and protect her from — again she halted in mid-thought. Protect her from what? What was it that suddenly made her feel frightened? It was absurd. She shook her head firmly. She was being nonsensical, she scolded herself. There was nothing threatening her.

As she turned to close the door behind her, the sound of footsteps on the stairs penetrated her consciousness. The door clicked shut and Elizabeth froze; the footsteps halted as well. Jed was midway up the stairs, a hand on the partially unknotted tie around his throat, the dark evening jacket swinging open. His tawny gaze held her captive and she felt threatened by the virility closing around her with suffocating strength.

Then Jed was pulling the tie the rest of the way free, letting it swing from his hand as he mounted the rest of the stairs. Elizabeth still didn't move, watching the unconscious grace of his movements. Not until she was again looking into his eyes, tilting her chin slightly upward now that he had reached the hallway, was she aware that she had waited for him and not retreated as she should have done.

His implacable gaze swung from her to the door she was standing in front of. 'Is Amy all right?'

'Yes.' Her answer was short and frayed. She was confused that she had waited. 'She's sleeping.'

Her fingers closed around the neckline of her robe, a defensive action although there had been no outward move from Jed to warrant it. A watchfulness crept into his lean, cynical features as he remained standing in front of her, making no move to continue down the hall to his room.

'What is it, Liza?' There was a drawling laziness to his voice, but it was a thin veil that concealed its sharpness. His eyes narrowed dangerously as she warily averted her gaze.

'I don't know what you're talking about,' she answered stiltedly, turning completely away in the direction of her room.

'Something's on your mind,' Jed prodded deliberately.

'If anything at all,' she kept her voice low so as not to disturb her sleeping daughter and worked to put chilling indifference in it, 'it's surprise to see you back so soon. I didn't expect you to be back until the morning.'

'Where did you think I'd be?' He drew in a deep,

impatient breath and exhaled it slowly in challenge as he spoke.

Hauteur made icicles in her voice. 'I didn't attempt to speculate what out-of-the-way place you and Barbara might choose.'

'I thought Barbara was your friend,' he drawled.

Irritation seethed in the flash of her accusing green eyes. 'She is,' Elizabeth snapped.

'Then why are you so indignant because I was friendly to her?' he mocked with harsh cynicism.

'Friendly?' she challenged coldly. 'You were very nearly making love to her on the dance floor. I'm not the only one who noticed.'

'What's it to you if I was?' He made no attempt to deny her accusation, a fact that further incensed Elizabeth.

'Because it was disgusting and contemptible to behave that way in public!' she retorted shrilly, then caught back the faintly hysterical tone in her voice. Lowering her head, she took a deep, calming breath. 'I found it extremely embarrassing. Your behavior was despicable.'

'And Barbara?' What about her behavior?' A cold smile was directed at her. 'She was hardly an innocent victim of unwanted advances,' he jeered.

Elizabeth refused to admit that much of the blame was Barbara's. 'I don't condone her behavior either.'

'What gives you the right to judge?' A contemptuous sound came from his throat and Elizabeth started toward her door. Jed jerked her around sharply, wrapping the tie around her neck and holding it beneath her chin with one hand. 'I can't make up my mind if you're frigid or just a prude.'

'Let go of me!' she ordered, her fingers closing around his wrist. The steel of his grip resisted her efforts to be free.

There was wild palpitation of her heart as Jed used the tie to draw her easily closer to him. The savage glitter in his gaze drove out the last of her poise. Her breath came in uneven gulps as he let his gaze dwell on her lips.

'I think it's time I found out,' he commented with analytical coolness.

The imprint of his hips was already making itself felt through the silkiness of her peignoir as Elizabeth arched herself away, pushing her hands against the solid wall of his chest. A frenzied sob of despair tore at her throat.

'You said you didn't want to touch me,' she reminded him frantically, as the tie bit into the back of her neck and pulled her inexplorably closer.

A thin smile twisted the hard line of his mouth. 'And that made you feel secure, didn't it? You felt safe in provoking me.' His male features taunted her foolishness. 'Did you forget who I am? I'm Jed, the worthless one, the black sheep. Haven't you learned that I'm not to be trusted?'

'No,' she pleaded weakly.

The tie around her neck and the hand under her chin wouldn't allow her to escape and his mouth covered hers in a series of slow, drugging kisses. Had he been bruising and fierce, she might have resisted, but his sensual possession was her undoing. She responded.

At some point the tie was discarded and his hands moulded the feminine softness of her form more fully aggainst the male hardness of his. The tidal wave of desire that carried her to dizzying heights exposed the raging core of passion within herself that not even she had known existed.

Her arms slipped beneath his jacket, circling the sinewy waist, the thin material of his white shirt like a second skin. The caress of his hands began an intimate exploration, too, that left her weak from the completeness of her response. She whimpered softly in protest when she felt the beginning withdrawal of his lips and clung to him more tightly.

'Damn,' Jed muttered softly in self-reproach, and she understood the reason. She had not wanted to feel this way about him either.

As he cupped her face in his hands and held her away, her lashes fluttered open to reveal luminous green eyes that were frightened by the depth of her desire for him and at the same time asking him to make the possession complete. Gold fires blazed in his eyes as he read the message in hers.

'Liza —' She hated the calm control that had entered his voice.

'Please,' she closed her eyes again, melting against him and nuzzling her cheek against the palm of his hand as a cat would prod the hand that had stopped stroking it, 'I don't want to talk.'

He allowed her to cuddle into his chest, his hands unconsciously caressing her shoulders and back. She had always guessed at the extent of his worldly expertise.

'A few minutes ago, you called me contemptible and disgusting.' His low voice taunted her with its cynical amusement. 'Am I supposed to feel honored now that you want me to make love to you?'

There was a stifled gasp of pain. 'Please!' An agonizing bubble in her throat choked off the rest of her protest.

'Please what?' His mouth moved along her temples. 'Please understand? Please forget all the insults? Please make love to me? What?' Jed prodded unmercifully.

'Don't be cruel,' Elizabeth murmured, a shame creeping in to steal her pleasure.

'I'm sorry, I feel cruel tonight,' he said harshly. 'I can't help it.'

His hands dug into her arms and pushed her away. It wasn't a genuine rejection because she knew he wanted her. She was not an inexperienced girl. She was a woman and she knew when she had aroused a man's desires. Still it hurt.

A tear quivered on the edge of her lash. Jed touched it, his forefinger catching it as it fell. Pride kept her gaze fixed on his impenetrable features, an aching need still pulsing through her body.

'I'm sorry, Liza,' he said again in a gentler yet just as firm tone. 'There really is such a thing as the right place and the right time. I thought I'd stopped wanting you, but I haven't.'

'Then why —' she started to ask huskily, but his finger touched her lips to silence them.

'Then why don't I take you?' He smiled wryly and sighed. As crimson heat colored her cheeks, he folded her gently into his arms. There was too much restraint in his embrace for her to draw any comfort or warmth. His voice vibrated with charged emotion near her ear. 'Because overriding my desire is a bitter violence,' he stated grimly.

'I don't understand.' Elizabeth had buried her face against his neck, now she raised it to gaze at him, bewilderedly.

'I know you don't.' The heady smile he bestowed on her didn't change the ruthless glint in his eyes. 'Maybe some day—' Jed hesitated. She felt him withdrawing from her, emotionally as well as physically, detaching himself from her arms with an impatient firmness. 'Good night, Elizabeth.'

Turning, he walked down the hall, not looking back once, not even when he walked through the door of his own room and closed it behind him. Empty and cold, Elizabeth stood where he had left her, wanting to follow him and frightened by the vague warning he had given her. Finally she went back to her own room and crawled into bed, her ears straining for some sound from his, but the walls of the old house were too thick.

She hadn't been certain what his attitude would be the following morning. He was such an enigma to her that she hadn't been able to guess whether he would silently mock the way she had thrown herself at him or pretend that it had never happened. She was uncertain what her own attitude should be.

Her own emotional upheaval was difficult to understand. She couldn't make up her mind whether she had been carried away by a wave of love or the backwash of sexual abstinence. In the end, she adopted a wait-and-see attitude and let Jed take the first step.

The first day there had been the crushing sensation that he was completely indifferent to her, aloofly so. The way he had of holding himself apart from others in their presence was more pronounced than ever. Then, that evening, she had felt his gaze dwelling on her with thoughtful, almost brooding intensity. He rarely addressed any comment to her, keeping the main flow of conversation with his mother, but neither did he subject her to any taunting jibes or mocking looks.

The waiting game was a difficult one for Elizabeth to play. Hope would alternately rise and fall until she felt she needed a barometer to record the erratic fluctuations. The physical attraction Jed held for her was undeniable. The most accidental contact had her senses leaping in immediate response. And she guessed that he had only to take her in his arms and she would be his for the asking.

Five days she went through the tortues of Tantalus. Jed's previous routine didn't vary much; he spent most of the day away from the house and some evenings. Yet there was never any pretense on his part that nothing had happened. The very second she thought there was, Jed would send her a look that was meant to remind her.

How much longer was this going to go on? Elizabeth

sighed to herself. Painstakingly she trimmed off the crust of the bread, varying the design of each slice from circles to squares to triangles. Flaky cherry tarts were cooling on the counter, the tarts and the canapés she was making were refreshments for Rebecca's Literary Club women. Their monthly meeting was being held here this time and Elizabeth had naturally been requested to take on the task of fixing the light refreshments.

'Can I help, Mom?' Elbows propped on the table, chin cradled in her hands, Amy glanced up at Elizabeth.

'May I help,' she corrected automatically. She pushed the small bowls of egg salad, ham salad and tuna salad to her daughter along with a knife. 'You can help me with the sandwiches.'

'*May* help,' Amy corrected her mother with impish humor.

A slow smile spread across Elizabeth's face as she ruefully nodded an acknowledgement of her own grammatical error. Cooking and preparing foods was another interest of Elizabeth's that Amy appeared to be beginning to share.

'How long are those ladies going to be here?' Amy asked in a less than enthusiastic tone.

'Probably until after four,' Elizabeth answered. At her daughter's grimace, she added, 'It would be best if you stayed in your room until it's time for the refreshments.'

'I suppose Mrs. Cargmore is going to be here,' Amy

grumbled, then adopted a mimicking voice. ' "Children should be seen and not heard." '

'At least not too often,' Jed added in conclusion.

The bread knife clattered to the floor, narrowly missing Elizabeth's foot as she spun around to face him. She tried to cover her confusion by bending to the floor to retrieve the knife, but in the next second Jed was kneeling beside her, handing her the knife. For all the amused mockery in his smile, his eyes were golden warm in her face.

'Someone should teach you to be careful with knives or you're going to end up chopping off your toe,' he scolded gently.

Her pulse was accelerating at an alarming pace. She straightened quickly, trying to hide the flow that brought an emerald brilliance to her eyes.

'You startled me,' she breathed in defense.

'Is that what I did?' Jed asked with a questing arch to one brow.

Bouncing her gaze away from his face, Elizabeth realized that he knew the way he disturbed her. He made a lazy, sweeping appraisal of her from head to toe, his eyes twinkling merrily when they returned to her face. She caught her breath at the change in his manner. The aloofness was gone, but what did it signify?

'All of this can't be for our consumption. Are we having a party?' Jed shifted his attention to the sandwiches Amy was stacking neatly on the plate.

'Not exactly,' Amy explained. 'Mom and I are doing the refreshments for Grandmother's Literary Club meeting.'

'Looks like I'll have to change my plans for the afternoon. I had thought I'd spend it around here, but not if we're about to be invaded.' The tobacco brown head made a definite negative shake.

'It isn't that bad,' Elizabeth murmured, her heart sinking slightly as she wished she knew if there was a particular reason why Jed had intended to spend the afternoon here — possibly with her? Was that what he had intended?

'Well, I sure wish I had somewhere else to go.' Amy licked the salad off her fingers and picked up another slice of bread.

'Amy, you shouldn't do that. Now wash your hands,' Elizabeth looked her reproval.

There was a disgruntled sigh as Amy replaced the knife and bread and walked to the sink. Jed was leaning against the counter, smiling faintly at Amy.

'So you've been condemned to spending the afternoon here?' he teased.

'In my room,' Amy answered with an expressive widening of her brown eyes. 'Isn't that exciting?'

'Well, you can always sit and count how many times Mrs. Garth sneezes,' he suggested dryly. 'That's what we used to do. Her record was twenty-four times as I recall.'

'Did you really count?' Amy giggled.

'Must you encourage her, Jed?' Elizabeth sighed, but with humor. 'Your mother already thinks she's disrespectful of her elders.'

'On second thoughts,' a smile played with the edges of his mouth, 'why don't you come with me this afternoon? I thought I'd visit Maggie.'

'Could we stop by the farm and see the puppies, too?'

'Amy, you —' The quick words of reproval were interrupted.

'Perhaps you should ask your mother if you can go,' Jed suggested.

Amy rebounded to Elizabeth, not allowing her time to bask in the faintly intimate smile he had turned to her. 'Please, Mom?'

'If Jed is sure he wants to take you, I don't object,' Elizabeth agreed. Her gaze was drawn back to the leanly carved face, less cynical now with its expression of patient indulgence, but no less compelling.

'Oh, he's sure, aren't you, Uncle Jed?' Amy hastened to have the invitation affirmed.

Jed straightened from the counter, the muscular length of him achieving his full height. Elizabeth felt the force of his masculinity drawing her to him even with the width of the table separating them.

'Yes, I'm sure,' he nodded. The grooves around his mouth deepened as he ruffled the top of Amy's head. 'I think we'd better be leaving before your grandmother discovers what we're up to and changes us into a couple of bookworms!'

Amy was already giggling and racing for the back door. Silently Elizabeth observed that her daughter seemed as anxious for Jed's company as she was. If only she could react that naturally and with such obvious pleasure instead of being plagued by uncertainty and caution!

'I'll look after her,' he said quietly, misinterpreting the slight frown.

'Of course,' Elizabeth smiled wanly, 'Thank you ... for asking her.'

Jed seemed to examine her words, his gaze running over her with disruptive thoroughness. Elizabeth was certain that her inner agitation must be apparent. Her shaky poise felt completely destroyed, assaulted by too many days of uncertaintly and doubt. But he made no comment regarding her stilted expression.

'We'll be back later this afternoon, with luck after the dragons have left,' he said, and followed the path Amy had blazed out of the door.

Staring after the lean figure, wide shoulders tapering to a slim waist and hips, Elizabeth wished they had asked her to come along. She couldn't have gone, of course, she acknowledged with a sigh, reverting her gaze to the bread slices on the cutting board. But she wished Jed had asked her for her company.

Luckily she didn't have to take part in the afternoon's meeting. As a silent participant, she was not required to concentrate on the book reviews being given. Once the meeting was over and the refreshments served, the women seemed to intend to linger indefinitely, exchanging local gossip. Mrs. Garth sneezed again and Elizabeth contained a smile.

This would never do, she told herself sternly. One more time and she would surely laugh aloud when she saw Mrs. Garth raising the embroidered handkerchief to her nose. As unobtrusively as possible, Elizabeth excused herself from the two ladies she had been sitting beside, guessing they would not miss her since she had added so little to the conversation, and began gathering together the dishes and carrying them to the kitchen.

On the third trip, she found Jed and Amy seated at the colonial kitchen table. Amy raised a conspiratorial finger of silence to her lips.

'Ssh!' she whispered. 'We don't want Grandmother to know we're back yet. Did she say anything?'

'Only that she hoped you'd behave yourself,' Elizabeth answered softly, not commenting on Rebecca's initial surprise and wary doubt on the advisability of letting Amy go with Jed. 'Did you have a nice time?'

'Oh, yes. Maggie was so glad to see me,' Amy asserted proudly. 'And Uncle Jed, too. And you should see the puppies, Mom! Freda said I could have one when they're old enough to leave their mother.'

'We'll see about that.' It was difficult to keep her gaze from straying too often to Jed. An odd breathlessness had claimed her lungs from the moment she had entered the room and encountered his tawny gaze. She carefully stacked the dishes in the sink, trying to control her schoolgirl reaction to his presence. 'There are some cherry tarts left. Would you two like some?'

'Yes, please,' Amy accepted eagerly, while Jed only nodded.

Just as Elizabeth set the plates with the tarts on the table in front of them, a sneeze echoed into the room.

Jed darted Amy a knowing look and smiled at her.

'There goes Mrs. Garth again,' he observed dryly.

Amy suppressed a giggle with her hand. 'How many times do you suppose that is?' she whispered gleefully.

'Seven—' Elizabeth bit quickly into her lip, suddenly and guiltily aware that she had been counting. Red flags of embarrassment ran up her cheeks at the mocking light in Jed's eyes.

'You've been counting!' Amy's brown eyes rounded in astonishment.

'Nonsense, I —' Her protest was defensively automatic, but the expressions on both their faces mirrored their disbelief.

'How many times, Liza?' Jed prompted softly.

Flustered for a second, Elizabeth turned back to the counter; their infectious humor was beginning to replace her chagrin. A smile hovered near the surface.

'Make her tell, Uncle Jed.' Checked laughter rippled through Amy's voice. 'I knew she was counting!'

At the scrape of the chair leg, Elizabeth glanced over her shoulder. At the sight of Jed's deliberate approach, her heart pattered wildly against her ribs.

'We shouldn't be making fun of Mrs. Garth this way,' she protested again. For too many years, her life had been ruled by strict courtesy for Elizabeth to succumb easily to their amused, yet innocent mockery. 'She can't help it.'

'How many, Liza?' A wide smile was daring her to continue to withhold the information.

Elizabeth pivoted to face him, her fingers closing over the hard counter top pushing into her back. 'It isn't polite.' Good judgment and discretion were rapidly being overtaken by the onslaught of his amused gaze.

'How many?' Jed persisted.

He was in front of her now; his nearness weakened her resistance. A smile started to break through and Elizabeth pressed her lips tightly together, glancing wildly at her daughter. But he had seen the laughter glittering in her green eyes. The touch of his hands on her shoulders brought it bubbling to the surface in soft giggles.

'Jed, Please!' It was a half-hearted protest through her laughter that acknowledged she was about to give in. Her palms spread across his chest in an effort to keep his intoxicating length at a safe distance.

Tilting back his head, he chuckled quietly in victory and drew her closer, locking his arms around her waist. 'You can't escape, Liza, until you tell us.'

'Seventeen.' Her answer was immediate and breathless.

Another sneeze was heard and they all broke into open laughter. Tears filled Elizabeth's eyes and she couldn't remember the last time she had laughed this hard. It was a wonderful, joyous sensation, especially since she was sharing it. Gradually it lessened into deep breaths for control. She found herself nestled under the crook of his arm, her head resting weakly against his shoulder.

Curving his hand under her chin, Jed raised it to inspect her face, and Elizabeth was much too contented and happy to do any more than gaze at his compellingly masculine features as he grinned at her.

'I've never seen you look more beautiful,' he murmured huskily, the gold light in his eyes burning over her face. 'You should laugh like that more often.'

'Really?' she whispered, basking in the fiery warmth, unable to decide whether the heat racing over her skin came from contact with him or was born inside herself.

'Yes, really.' Although there was mocking amusement in his voice, it wasn't the message she saw written in his gaze as he slowly turned her into his arms, his hands moving in an arousing caress down her shoulders and spine to mold her closer against him.

A tiny sound from the table reminded Elizabeth suddenly that they were not alone. Amy was watching them with obvious interest. Quickly she averted her head from Jed's descending mouth, gasping slightly as he settled on the lobe of her ear.

'Jed, please,' she whispered with a self-conscious glance at her round-eyed daughter. 'N-not in front of Amy.'

He lifted his head a few inches from hers in seeming discretion, a crooked smile twisting the sensually male lips. The glitter of his eyes never left her face.

'Amy, do I have your permission to kiss your mother?' he asked quietly. The grooves around his mouth deepened at the rush of pink in Elizabeth's cheeks.

'Yes,' Amy answered quickly with a broad, conspiring look, and settled into her chair to watch.

'You see?' he mocked.

This time he didn't take any chances that Elizabeth might avoid his kiss, but held her chin firmly until he had taken possession of her mouth. At his masterful touch, she surrendered to the whirl of inevitability, letting the waves break over her head and become submerged in the superior force of his attraction.

A horrified gasp broke through the ardency that was about to carry Elizabeth completely away. As she broke away from the addictive pressure of his lips, her startled gaze encountered the shocked faces of three members of the Literary Club. At her twisting turn, Jed partially released her from their embrace, keeping one hand firmly around her waist and in plain view of the ladies. Before he glanced at the trio, his gaze mocked Elizabeth's crimsoning complexion.

'Was there something you ladies wanted?' he inquired with unbelievable calm.

'We were just leaving,' one of them sniffed.

'We thought we should see Elizabeth and offer our goodbye,' a second responded, a brow arching at Elizabeth in disapproval.

The third woman merely looked from Elizabeth to the gleaming Amy and back to Elizabeth. Her indignant shock was more condemning in its silence than the rest. Stiffly Elizabeth thanked them for coming.

The three women were barely out of the kitchen before the rapid exchange of their voices could be heard, no doubt comparing reactions. Only then did Jed remove his hand from her waist, lighting a cigarette from his picket and letting his contemplative gaze dwell on the uncomfortable warmth still reddening her face.

'Does it bother you that you're going to be the subject of a lot of talk?' His tone challenged despite the softness of his question.

'Yes,' Elizabeth swallowed. 'It does a little.'

'Jeremy was always the apple of the town's eye, not me. Are you ashamed to be seen with me?'

Her gaze bounced away from the harshness in his otherwise calm expression. 'Not ashamed,' she hedged. 'I would have been self-conscious with anyone.'

Jed studied her face for a long moment. The expression in his own masculine features was unrelenting. Then he turned to walk away.

'Jed.' Her whispered plea called for his understanding.

Without glancing back, he paused beside her daughter's chair, and Elizabeth noted the faint softening of his profile as he gazed into Amy's curious and concerned expression.

'Your mother is a prude, Amy,' he smiled crookedly.

'Is that bad?' Amy breathed.

There was a resigned shrug of his shoulders that was hardly encouraging as it accompanied the negative shake of his head. 'No, it isn't bad.' Then glancing briefly at Elizabeth he added, 'I'll be back for dinner,' and left from the rear door of the kitchen.

CHAPTER SEVEN

'Is that everything, Mrs. Carrel?' The woman clerk paused before ringing up the total on the cash register.

'Yes, thank you,' Elizabeth responded, absently glancing to be certain that Amy was still at her side.

'It's quite a chore getting children ready for school these days. The list of things they need keeps getting longer and longer,' the woman sighed. 'With five of my own in school, I ought to be an expert on it.'

'I think this completes Amy's list.' Elizabeth smiled as she took the smaller of the two parcels and handed it to her daughter, juggling the larger into a comfortable position with her two previous purchases.

'Are you ready for school to start?' The clerk smiled down at Amy.

'I suppose so,' she shrugged.

'I thought you were looking forward to the first day of school?' Elizabeth tilted her ebony dark head in curious surprise.

'Not since Unce Jed came back. It's much more fun at home now that he's there,' Amy observed.

'Uncles usually are more fun than school,' the clerk agreed, darting an amused look at Elizabeth.

'Jed is fun. He even makes Mom laugh,' asserted Amy.

Another customer approached the check-out counter and Elizabeth was relieved to direct her talkative daughter toward the door. The clerk's look of amusement ha d been tinged by speculation after Amy's last comment. There was little doubt in Elizabeth's mind that the incident witnessed by the three members of the Literary Club had been transmitted all over town.

A faint sigh of frustration slipped from her throat as she and Amy stepped outside. Truthfully she had expected Jed to seek her out again, but over the weekend not once had he indicated that he wanted to be alone with her. He had been charming and amusing, as Amy had pointed out, but he had also avoided any opportunity to be alone with her.

'Good morning, Elizabeth. We seemed destined to meet on the sidewalks of Carrelville. Good morning, Amy.'

Focusing her gaze on the man who had stopped in front of them, Elizabeth realized that she hadn't even noticed Allan approaching them.

'Hello, Allan. How are you?' Her words of greeting were falsely warm to cover the initial blank look she had given him.

'Fine,' he nodded. 'Looks like you've been doing a little shopping.'

'We've been getting Amy's things for school,' she explained.

'It's getting close to that time,' Allan agreed. He addressed the observation to Amy, but she was gazing about them with obvious lack of interest toward the man now talking to her mother. There was a hint of firmness in the smile he turned to Elizabeth and she knew he was irritated by Amy's attitude, one that she echoed at this minute but was too polite to let show. 'I was just on my way to the restaurant for morning coffee. Would you two care to join me?'

'I'm not old enough to drink coffee.' Amy scuffed the toe of her shoe on the sidewalk before turning cold brown eyes toward his face.

'How about milk and doughnuts, then?' Allan suggested with thinning patience.

Elizabeth's own polite words of refusal were checked. She was no more enthusiastic about having coffee with Allan than Amy was, but her daughter's churlishness had been cuttingly rude. Allan had always been kind and considerate. He didn't deserve that kind of treatment.

'That sounds like an excellent idea,' she accepted warmly, sending a warning look to Amy, whose mouth was opening in protest. Her mouth went grimly shut as she tucked her chin into her neck and glowered at the sidewalk. 'Our car is just across the street. We'll put our packages in there and join you.'

'Let me help you carry some of that,' Allan offered.

'They're not at all heavy,' Elizabeth assured him as he fell into step beside them as if to make sure they didn't change their mind once they were at their car. 'Besides, I have them balanced in such a manner that if you took one, they would all fall.'

At the intersection, they waited for the light to change. Elizabeth made a polite inquiry about the hospital and half listened to his reply. Across the street a set of broad shoulders looked achingly familiar. A second later, the man turned away from the shop window and the sharply etched profile confirmed it was Jed. Another second later, Elizabeth recognized Barbara, curling her arms through Jed's and hugging close to him as they started down the street toward the same intersection she was waiting to cross.

Pain gnawed at her stomach walls. Jealousy had always been an alien emotion. Now she felt its tortuous grip and its sickening side effects. She tried to swallow back the nauseating lump in her throat, without success.

Do you see? a malicious voice whispered in her ear. Do you see the way he's accepting the attention as if it was his due? That's what he wants from you. He'd like to add you to his string of conquests. Once he's got you to fall in love with him, do you think he'll marry you? He's not the marrying kind, the hideous voice reminded her.

'Look, Mom!' Amy cried excitedly. 'There's Uncle Jed!' And she waved the paper sack in her hand to attract Jed's attention.

Glancing away from the blonde molded to his side, Jed saw them. A frown of displeasure darkened his face, the lean hard features still compellingly handsome. Tears of irritation and pride blurred Elizabeth's vision. She had just as much right as he had to be in town, she told herself bitterly.

The light at the intersection changed. With a proud toss of her head she started across, but the watery collection of tears in her green eyes had affected her perception. She misjudged the distance from the curb to the pavement and stumbled. The packages spewed from her arms as she released them to try to check her fall. She wasn't even aware that she had cried out nor saw Allan's arms reaching out to try to catch her.

Winded and stunned, she lay unmoving on the pavement for a few seconds to try to collect her wits. She smiled weakly at Allan as he bent anxiously beside her and pushed herself into a sitting position.

'Are you all right?' he frowned, making a quick examination of the graze on her elbow.

Elizabeth nodded, unable to speak, partly from shock and partly from humiliation. Her fall had drawn everyone's attention and they were gathered in a tight circle around her.

'Stand back. Give her some room,' a familiar voice was ordering crisply, and the people were obeying as Jed pushed his way through. Elizabeth studiously brushed the dust from her cranberry skirt, avoiding the gold sharpness of his eyes. Her heartbeat became erratic when he knelt beside her. 'Are you hurt, Liza?'

'I — I'm all right,' Elizabeth murmured, trying to withdraw her grazed elbow from Jed's hold.

'She fell down,' Amy explained.

'So I noticed,' Jed murmured dryly, completely ignoring Allan who hovered to one side, his position usurped by the firm authority that had accompanied Jed's arrival. 'Is your middle name Grace?'

The pink intensified in her cheeks. 'I simply misjudged the step.'

'Did you twist your ankle?' His fingers scorched an inquisitive trail along her shinbone to her ankle.

'I may not be a practising physician, but I am a doctor,' Allan inserted sharply, trying to reassert his position as Elizabeth's rescuer.

'And I've probably treated more injuries and illnesses than you have,' Jed snapped. Evidently satisfied that there was no indication of a sprain, he slipped a supporting arm around her waist. 'Let's get you on your feet.'

'I'm all right,' Elizabeth repeated.

'Heavens, Jed, there isn't anything wrong with her,' Barbara cut in. 'Allan can take care of her.'

The blonde's comment wasn't even acknowledged as Jed lifted Elizabeth to her feet. She didn't know whether to blame the light headedness on the fall or the steel band holding her so close to his lean, muscular hips and thighs. The malevolent dislike in Barbara's cold blue eyes did make her reel instinctively toward Jed in search of protection. His arms tightened around her.

'I'll carry you to the car,' he stated, sliding his other arm under the back of her legs and easily swinging her off her feet.

Unfortunately for the man standing toward the back of the crowd, the faint buzz of concerned voices stopped just as he murmured to a friend, 'I bet he's carried her to far more intimate and comfortable places than that!''

A rigid stillness entered Jed's features as dangerous cat-gold eyes narrowed unerringly on the man who had made the jeering comment. The ruthless set of his jaw was intimidating. Elizabeth shivered uncontrollably when he slowly lowered her to her feet.

'I believe you owe the lady an apology, Mick.' Jed spoke with ominous softness.

'I didn't mean anything by it, Jed.' The man named Mick shifted uncomfortably, as the crowd parted between the two men.

The air crackled, invisible electricity snapping at coiled nerves. The arm Jed had kept around her waist was a suffocating iron band. Elizabeth knew he wasn't aware of the force he was applying. She also knew Jed wouldn't relent from his stand until the man had apologized for his slighting remark.

'Please.' Jed paid no notice to her request for his attention, so Elizabeth turned to Mick. 'There's no need for you to apologize,' she insisted with quiet pride. 'You were only voicing the suspicions of everyone here in this town. I can't expect you to be the only one to apologize.'

'I'm sorry, Mrs. Carrel.' His gaze skittered across her face to Jed's and fell away.

'Here's your packages, Mrs. Carrel.' Another one of the group stepped forward to hand her the packages that had fallen to the street.

Jed took them before Elizabeth had a chance, giving one to Amy. 'You're big enough to carry this.' The other he retained while keeping an arm firmly circling Elizabeth's waist. She couldn't very well protest without causing more comment. Besides, she partially welcomed his strong support.

'Elizabeth, let me take you to the hospital,' Allan offered quietly. 'You should have those grazes cleaned and disinfected.'

The crowd had begun to thin, the excitement over. The sting in her scraped elbows was becoming more pronounced, but Elizabeth's only wish was to leave — as quickly as possible.

'It's really not necessary,' she refused with a weakly polite smile.

'They should be taken care of,' he reiterated.

'I'll see to it,' Jed said firmly. His jaw was still clenched, the savage anger not yet fully abated.

'What about me?' Barbara demanded.

'I'll see you later.' The light had changed again and Jed was pushing Amy to start across the street to the car, not at all concerned or interested in Barbara's indignant outburst.

'I might be busy,' she retorted haughtily.

Except for a cynical twist of his mouth, there was no reaction from Jed as he began half carrying, half guiding Elizabeth across the street. Secretly Elizabeth thought he was mocking Barbara's boldly false statement that she might reject him. It was disturbing to acknowledge that he was right. There were very few women who wouldn't take him back. And she had the dreadful feeling she was among them, and it was a severe blow to her pride.

'Well, you've done it now, little miss diplomat,' Jed snapped as he slammed the car door shut. 'Where are the keys?'

Elizabeth fumbled nervously through her bag and

126

handed them to him. Huddling next to the door, she heard the motor spring to life, growling with all the suppressed power of its driver.

'I didn't do anything wrong. Unless you call avoiding a fight wrong?' she challenged defensively.

'Whether you like it or not, you've been labeled as *my* property.' As they left the city limits, he accelerated until the car was whizzing by the telephone poles at an alarming rate.

'What does that mean?' Amy leaned forward over Elizabeth's seat.

But Elizabeth chose to ignore the question. 'If I have, it's due just as much to your actions,' she retorted.

'Because I chose to take offence on your behalf at that man's remarks?' Jed mocked, quirking a brow briefly in her direction. 'Did it ever occur to you that I might have been defending your "good name," ' there was a definite sarcasm in the last, 'as my sister-in-law and not as —' He glanced in the back seat to Amy's expression of round-eyed interest and didn't finish the sentence.

'What does it mean, Momma? How can you be Uncle Jed's property? I thought you couldn't own people?' Amy persisted, taking advantage of the slight lull in the conversation.

'You can't own people,' Elizabeth replied with brittle patience.

'Then what does it mean?'

'It's like going steady, Amy,' Jed answered this time with the same controlled tone. 'We aren't supposed to date anyone else but each other. That's what I mean.''

'Mom can't go out with anyone but you? Not even Mr. Marsden?'

'That's right,' Jed clipped.

'Good!' Amy declared with one vigorous nod of satisfaction. 'I don't like him very much.'

'Amy!' Elizabeth's outcry was automatic.

But Jed had thrown his head back and was laughing. The deep, hearty sound was contagious. It played with the corners of Elizabeth's mouth until she too began laughing.

'Oh, Amy!' Jed shook his head with a sobering sigh as he turned the car into the house lane. 'You're a treasure. Let's get your mother's arm fixed up, then see if we can persuade your grandmother to let us have lunch outside.'

'Like a picnic? Terrific!' Amy agreed. 'But Grandmother hates to eat outside. There's too many bugs.

'No worry,' Elizabeth was still smiling. 'Your grandmother won't be here for lunch today. It's—' An expression of dismay swept across her face. 'Oh, Amy, it's Thursday! Your piano lesson.'

'Oh, Mom, no!' Amy wailed.

'Come on, Liza.' Jed switched the motor off and turned to her. 'What's one piano lesson in a lifetime of piano lessons?' he chided gently. 'Call her teacher and tell her the car won't start.'

'Please, Mom,' Amy echoed, adding her persuasions to those of her advocate.

'What if we eat later after your piano lesson?' Elizabeth suggested. 'You can skip practising this time

128

and we'll still have our lunch outdoors, if you like."

'Instead of that,' Jed countered, 'why don't you let Amy practise for half an hour while you're getting lunch and skip the lesson?'

'Wouldn't that be just as good, Mom, please?'

'Well, all right,' Elizabeth agreed finally, glowing a bit under the admiring wink Jed bestowed on her. Amy's shriek of gladness forced her to add a cautioning note, 'But only if you practise for half an hour.'

'I will!' her daughter promised fervently, pushing open the door and hopping out of the car. 'I'll start right now.'

She was ready to race for the house when Jed whistled her to a stop. 'Don't go in empty-handed,' he told her. 'Take one of the packages.'

Grabbing one of the packages from the back seat, Amy was careering toward the front door again, not waiting for Jed and Elizabeth. He tucked the remaining two packages under his arm and stepped from the car when Elizabeth did.

'You would have thought I'd given her the moon,' she smiled ruefully after her daughter.

'Playing hookey is always fun, even if you have permission.' His lazy smile was captivating as he fell into step beside her.

'I've heard you were an expert at playing hookey,' she teased.

'I probably was absent as much as I was present,' he admitted with a twinkle. "Absolutely incorrigible" was the way the truant officer described me. I'm not exactly proud of it, but I probably learned earlier than most how to apply what school had taught me to the realities of living.'

'I remember,' Elizabeth murmured with a flash of recall, 'your father once said that you had a very analytical and logical mind and that you could have been a brilliant lawyer if you weren't so —' she hesitated.

'Incorrigible,' he supplied mockingly. 'When did he make that concession that I might possibly have some brains?'

'Shortly after Jeremy was killed.' He held the front door open for her. 'I think he was really hoping you would come back then.'

'To his way of life.' There was a bitter, downward twist to his mouth. 'Come on, let's get your arm cleaned.'

'I'm sure he only wanted what he thought was best for you,' she murmured.

'I have no doubt he meant well.' Jed motioned her toward a kitchen chair and walked to the cabinet where the first-aid kit was kept. 'I forgave him for his intentions a long time ago. The trouble is he never forgave me for choosing my own style of life.'

In the next instant, antiseptic was burning the scrape on her elbow. Her quickly drawn gasp of pain brought an apologetic smile, but Jed continued until it was clean. By then the conversation was forgotten and Amy was faithfully at the piano practising.

While Jed disappeared to wash, Elizabeth telephoned Mrs. Banks, Amy's piano teacher. Thankfully the woman accepted her explanation. Elizabeth hadn't pretended any car trouble, merely stating that Amy wouldn't be keeping her lesson today.

Working in the kitchen had always been satisfying to her, but she discovered there was a special contentment within as she set about fixing the noon meal for just the three of them. When she spied Jed standing on the patio, she realized it was the way she wanted it to be for always.

The depth of her love for the lean, virile man standing out there frightened her. She knew she had jumped into very deep water. For the present Jed was holding on to her. But what would she do if he ever let go? With Jeremy, she had only been playing in the shallows. Now she was in over her head.

Elizabeth turned from the window, fighting back the panic that nearly sent her racing to Jed's arms seeking some reassurance that he cared with more than just physical passion. The agonizing pain of the morning was vividly recalled, that twisting, sickening jealousy when she had seen him with Barbara. And Barbara expected to see him again today.

It was difficult to regain the sensation of contentment. Tensely Elizabeth waited all through lunch for the moment Jed would say he was going. While she cleared the table, Amy persuaded him to play a game of croquet. Elizabeth sensed that behind his laughter and his teasing conversation with her daughter, his mind was thinking of something or someone else. It was difficult to know if it was her imagination.

The game was over with Jed the winner when Elizabeth finished washing up the lunch dishes. She brought a fresh pitcher of lemonade with her as she returned to the patio. Jed was just leaning back in one of the lounge chairs when he saw her.

'You read my mind,' he smiled lazily. 'We'll drink that whole pitcherful before this afternoon is over. It's going to be hot.'

She steadied her shaking hand as she poured him a glass. 'What about Barbara?' Elizabeth tried to sound nonchalant.

'What about her?' After wiping the beads of perspiration from his forehead, he took the glass, sipping it appreciatively.

'Isn't she expecting you this afternoon?'

He ran an amused eye over her face, as if sensing the underlying urgency in her question. 'It wasn't anything definite.' He leaned his head back against the cushion, running the ice-cold glass along his temple. 'Besides, it's too hot to play tennis this afternoon.'

'Is that what you were going to do?' Elizabeth murmured.

'What did you think?' Jed mocked, examining her downcast gaze over the brim of his glass.

'I didn't think,' she answered, looking anywhere but at him. She didn't actually believe Barbara planned to play tennis all afternoon and certainly not if she had Jed all to herself.

'Liar,' he taunted. 'I think I detected a tint of jealous green in your eyes just then.'

'You . . . you must have been imagining it.'

'That's a pity.' Jed closed his eyes against the sun, amusement teasing the corners of his mouth. 'Since I made my preference for the company of the young widow Carrel and her daughter instead of the pleasures of her friend so obvious, I foolishly hoped she might unbend from her straightlaced ways enough to admit that she wanted mine.'

The gaze she had kept averted swung to him sharply, afraid he might be mocking her again and praying that he was speaking the truth. With his eyes still closed, Jed reached out with his hand and found the fingers that were clutching the arm of her chair. Slowly, the brown curling lashes were raised and the enigmatic gold lights in his eyes were focused on her wary face.

'It's true, Liza,' he said evenly and naturally.

Her heart quickened at his touch. 'Why?' she asked breathlessly, still questioning whether he was playing with her emotions.

'Why do you think?' There was a husky seductive quality to his countering question that sent fire through her veins.

'Let's play another game of croquet!' Amy came bounding between the two chairs, breaking the magic spell that Jed had been casting over her.

'It's too hot,' he smiled his protest.

'Come on,' Amy pleaded, taking both their hands and tugging to get them to rise to their feet.

'One game,' Jed surrendered.

Amy was delighted to have both her uncle and her

mother apparently at her disposal for the entire afternoon. Her constant presence negated any opportunity for the conversation to return to its former personal note, a fact that Elizabeth didn't know whether to be thankful for or regret. An inner perception told her that she would never find out more than Jed wanted her to know. While she — was she being blatantly transparent about her own feelings?

Under the present circumstances of uncertainty, it was ironic how innocently confident she had been when she had set out to capture Jeremy. From the first time she had met him, she had been determined to marry him. Had it ever been love? When the accident had taken him, it had been shock rather than grief she had felt. She had been an immature young girl seeking the fantasty of love. Now she was a mature woman and the eyes with which she beheld Jed were those of a woman in the thralls of a mature, profound love.

She was allowing her imagination to carry her away, she scolded herself sternly. It was a beautiful day. She should be enjoying it and stop looking around every corner for some impending disaster.

'What's the frown for?' Jed tilted his head inquiringly, his thick brown hair gleaming in the afternoon sun. Before Elizabeth had a chance to answer him, he glanced toward the house. 'Ah, Mother's home,' he sighed. 'She does inhibit people.'

Elizabeth turned as Rebecca stepped through the French doors from the living room. 'There you are. It's terribly hot out here, isn't it?' she greeted them, her dark gaze swept over the three of them, nodding briefly in response to the greetings.

'It is a bit warm,' Elizabeth agreed.

Rebecca Carrel's attention focused on her. 'I heard you had a slight accident today, Elizabeth.'

For an instant Elizabeth held her breath. She hadn't dreamed today's episode would be relayed to her mother-in-law so quickly.

'A scrape on the elbow. Nothing serious,' she shrugged.

'How convenient Jed was there to take care of you,' Rebecca murmured, swinging her sharp gaze to her son.

The cat-gold glitter returned in answer to the silent challenge of her eyes. "If I hadn't been there, there were plenty of volunteers who would have seen to it that Elizabeth was all right.'

'Well, at least you look none the worse for this mishap.' The saccharine smile did little to soften the haughty features. 'Was there anything you would like me to help you cook for dinner this evening?'

'No,' Elizabeth refused stiffly. 'I was going to put a roast in the oven. I . . . I think I'll start it now.'

She was nearly to the french doors when she heard foot-steps behind her, strong quiet strides that belonged to Jed. She turned, trying to fight away the awkwardness Rebecca's arrival had induced.

'I meant to tell you earlier,' Jed stopped beside her, drawing the french doors shut behind him, 'I won't be home for dinner this evening.'

'Of course,' her frozen voice acknowledged, chilled by the cold hand that gripped her heart. He hadn't seen Barbara this afternoon because he intended to see her tonight.

'Of course?' A curious, amused frown creased his forehead. 'Why do you say, "of course"?'

'There was no special significance,' she lied. 'It was merely an acknowledgment.'

'Have it your way, Liza,' he smiled mockingly, and walked toward the stairway.

How she despised Barbara at that moment! She could have cheerfully clawed her eyes out if she had been there. Jealousy was an ugly thing.

CHAPTER EIGHT

IT was the second cup of coffee she had stared at until it got cold, Elizabeth thought resentfully as she poured it down the sink. If she wasn't so angry at herself for being so foolish to believe that Jed might care about her, she would be crying.

Yesterday afternoon he had said that he wouldn't be home for supper. She had lain awake in her bed until well after midnight, feeling miserably sorry for herself before drifting off to restless sleep with out having heard Jed return. With good reason! He hadn't returned!

After the first angrily jealous shock had receded, fear had set in. There could have been an accident. She had frantically dialled the police to see if an accident had been reported, terror filling her heart that she might have lost Jed as she had Jeremy. But none had. Nor had he been admitted to the local hospital. That left only one place for him to be — with Barbara.

Tears scalded her cheeks and she scrubbed them away with her hand. She was not going to cry because of her own stupidity. She should have had more sense than to fall in love with someone like Jed. The bitter taste of her love nearly gagged her.

The front doorbell rang. Who could that possibly be at this hour of the morning, she thought angrily. She was in no mood to entertain any visitor for Rebecca. The coffee cup clattered against the side of the porcelain sink as the doorbell sounded impatiently again.

Smoothing her hair away from her face and breathing deeply, Elizabeth walked through the kitchen into the hall, her nerves stretched to screaming pitch. She wanted to release their tension when the doorbell rang again. The smile on her face was less than welcoming as she opened the door.

'Freda?' She identified the young woman standing outside in surprise. 'What are you doing here?'

Freda Reisner's hands twisted nervously in front of her. 'Jed —' she began hesitantly.

Elizabeth immediately stiffened. 'I'm sorry, he isn't here this morning.'

'I . . . I know he isn't,' Freda faltered under the chilling coldness that underlined Elizabeth's reply. 'He's at our farm.'

'At your farm?' Elizabeth repeated bewilderedly. 'I thought he was — Is he hurt? Has there been an accident?'

'There wasn't an accident.' Freda shook her dark blonde head quickly to banish that fear. 'But I'm afriad he's ill.'

'Oh, my God!' Elizabeth whispered, covering her trembling mouth and chin with her hand.

'He had supper with us last night and fell asleep on the couch. Then later . . . he was ill,' Freda explained. 'He made Kurt promise not to tell you.'

'Have you called a doctor?'

'Yes, before I came over, but Jed refused to go to the hospital. Maybe he'll listen to you,' Freda sighed.

138

'May I drive over with you?' Elizabeth requested anxiously. 'Of course.' Freda Reisner turned away from the door, hurrying down the sidewalk to her waiting pick-up truck.

'Amy! Amy!' Elizabeth called to her daughter playing in the back of the house. She had barely explained to her the cause for her alarm before she was hurrying into the truck and Freda was reversing out of the drive.

The doctor's car was already at the Reisner farm when they arrived. Elizabeth recognized it as belonging to their family doctor which probably accounted for the fact that Freda was able to get him to come out.

'Where is he?' Elizabeth glanced at Freda, unwilling to blindly follow the sound of muttering male voices.

'In the downstairs bedroom, second door on the right in the hall,' Freda pointed.

'Stay here with Freda, Amy,' Elizabeth requested, and pivoted in the direction Freda had indicated.

Pausing in the open doorway, she stared at the man lying in the double bed, a fist pressed against her stomach. There was a sickly sallow color making itself seen beneath the darkness of Jed's tanned face. Perspiration gleamed on his forehead and above his upper lip. The tawny-colored eyes were closed, but she guessed from weakness rather than sleep. Her gaze swung to the tall, stoop-shouldered man who had just taken Jed's pulse.

'How is he?' Apprehension made her voice one degree above a whisper.

'Ah, Elizabeth,' the doctor smiled. 'Kurt said you and Rebecca were probably on your way over.'

At the sound of her voice, Jed moved slightly, lashes fluttering open to focus on Elizabeth. Resentment filtered through the glaze of fever dominating his gold-flecked eyes when he glanced at the second man standing near his bedside.

'Rebecca didn't come,' Elizabeth murmured, trying to return the smile of encouragment Kurt Reisner was giving her. 'She's in town at a meeting of some sort.' Her mother-in-law's whereabouts were of little concern to her at the moment. Each beat of her heart was for a previously vital man lying so listlessly on the bed. 'Jed — what's wrong — with him?'

The doctor cast a faintly amused glance at Jed before moving slowly toward Elizabeth. 'This is one case where I'm accepting the patient's diagnosis.' Again there was the reassuring smile that there was no need for alarm. 'He picked up a fever in the tropics, and he tells me that he has had recurring bouts of it before. A couple of days and it'll run its course. In the meantime, he'll be a sick man, but he assures me there are no lasting effects.'

'Shouldn't he go to the hospital?' she suggested anxiously, not as convinced as the doctor that there was no cause for alarm.

'No.' The hoarsely weak and angry protest came from Jed.

The doctor chuckled softly. 'As you can see, he's very much against that. The hospital is a bit cramped for space right now and a s long as his temperature .stays at a manageable level, I see no reason to admit him.'

'Can he be moved?' Another strangled protest came

from the bed, but Elizabeth ignored it. 'I'd like to take him home if it's all right.'

'He's more than welcome to stay here,' Kurt spoke up. 'He won't be that much of a burden for a few days. If he is,' there was a darting look of amusement at Jed, 'we'll simply throw him out.'

It was the doctor's opinion that mattered. Elizabeth wanted Jed home where she could look after him.

'It probably wouldn't hurt him to be moved,' the doctor hesitated, glancing from Elizabeth to Jed and back. 'If the Reisners are willing to take care of him, it would be best if he stayed here. No sense running the risk of any outside complications.'

'Of course,' Elizabeth accepted his verdict grudgingly.

'I'd better be getting to the hospital.' The doctor pushed back the sleeve of his jacket to look at his watch. 'I still have my rounds to make.' Glancing at Kurt, he asked, 'You have that prescription I gave you?'

Kurt touched the pocket of his shirt. 'Yes.' He glanced briefly at Elizabeth, then walked to the doctor's side. 'I'll show you to the door.'

Discreetly left alone in the room with Jed, Elizabeth found herself uncertain what to say or do next. His eyes were closed again. Awkwardly she moved closer to the bed, wanting to touch him, to reassure herself that her fear was unwarranted, but she was loath to disturb him.

A bowl of water and a cloth were on the table beside the bed. As quietly as possible, Elizabeth moistened the cloth, folded it into a swuare and gently placed it on his forehead. There was a tightness in the region of her heart as she gazed at his lean features, in repose yet finely drawn into taut lines. Her green eyes mirrored the suffering that she sensed was concealed behind the controlled impassivity of his expression. When she removed the cloth to moisten it again with the cool water, she saw his eyes open. She tried to camouflage her inner anxiety with brisk movements.

'It's the young widow Carrel, soothing my fevered brow,' he mocked weakly.

'Be quiet,' she commanded softly, watching his eyes close as she placed the damp cloth on his forehead.

'Go home, Elizabeth,' Jed mumbled coldly. 'I don't need you.' He pushed her hand away, but not with his former strength. There's no one to see you. There's no need to keep up any appearances.'

Calmly Elizabeth returned the cloth to his forehead as if to pretend that his cutting words hadn't sliced deeply. She made no reply, persevering in her attempt to do something to relieve his discomfort, and Jed uttered no more protests, but slipped into a troubled sleep.

Quiet footsteps entered the room. Their feminine lightness made it easy for Elizabeth to identify them as belonging to Freda before she turned around.

'Is he sleeping?' Freda asked.

'I think it's something in between.' The corners of her mouth turned upward in a weak example of a smile as she placed the cloth on the side of the bowl.

'I've just made a fresh pot of coffee. Would you like a cup?'

Casting one last look at Jed, Elizabeth nodded. 'Yes, I would.'

There was no sign of Amy in the kitchen. Freda read

the question forming in Elizabeth's eyes and answered, 'Amy's outside playing with the puppies.'

'I'm —' Elizabeth ran a hand nervously through the side of her hair, the black locks curling about her fingers. 'I'm sorry we've put you to so much trouble, Freda.'

'It isn't any trouble,' the dark blonde assured her, setting a mug of coffee on the table for each of them. 'Jed has been like a second brother to Kurt and me ever since I can remember. My mother swore that he spent more time at our place than he ever did at home, but I don't think his parents knew that.'

'Yes, well,' Elizabeth sighed heavily, 'I'm afraid he'll be here for a few more days. Doctor Miles didn't think it was a good idea to move him, at least for the time being. Jed didn't seem anxious to leave either.'

'Nor would anyone if they were ill,' Freda defended him gently.

'Still, I wish —' Elizabeth glanced toward the hallway and the hidden bedroom door, but she couldn't put into words the compelling need to be the one who took care of him. 'It's such an inconvenience for you,' she murmured instead.

'Elizabeth —' Freda began, then hesitated, giving undue interest to the coffee in her mug. 'If you would like to stay and lend a hand, I would appreciate it. I mean, I do have the house to take care of and the meals to cook for Kurt and there's a lot of work in the garden to be done. You could sleep in the spare room unless you'd rather not.'

'Are you sure you wouldn't object?' Elizabeth held

her breath, wanting to stay with Jed more than anything.

'It would be a tremendous help,' Fred promised.

'I would like to stay.' Elizabeth's smile was genuine this time, a mixture of happiness and relief.

'The spare room has twin beds. There's no reason Amy can't stay, too. I know your mother-in-law,' Freda seemed to choose her words carefully, 'is quite busy with her meetings and all. It would save you from having to find a sitter and constantly rushing back and forth between our two places. And she isn't any trouble.'

'Oh, Freda, are you sure you want us Carrels to invade you this way?' Elizabeth laughed.

'I'm sure,' Freda nodded with a beaming smile. 'As soon as Kurt comes back in from the field at noon, I'll have him drive you over to the house to get your things. It's a perfect arrangement.'

The only one who disapproved of the arrangement was Rebecca. It was her opinion that if Jed was ill enough to require Elizabeth's attention, he was ill enought to be in hospital. For once, Elizabeth didn't allow herself to be talked out of her plans, not even when her mother-in-law insisted that Amy should remain at home with her. The tiny wedge that had been driven between them since Jed's arrival had placed a severe strain on the relationship between the two women. Elizabeth found that she didn't look up to her mother-in-law as much as she once had. In fact there were several things about her that she didn't like.

Amy was delighted at the prospect of possibly spending several days on the Reisner farm. She was genuinely concerned that her uncle was ill, but it didn't diminish her delight. The farm was a new world to her, an exciting world that she was determined to explore.

When Kurt had heard his sister's suggestion, he immediately added his second to the invitation, adding that he knew Freda would enjoy the company of someone her own age. And Elizabeth discovered how very warm and friendly her neighbors truly were. She felt ashamed that she hadn't followed her instinct and got to know them better before now. But Rebecca had never been in favor of Elizabeth becoming too closely acquainted with them.

Although she could ignore her mother-in-law's disapproval, Jed's displeasure at having her there was not so easy to overlook. Several times during the first day, Elizabeth sat with him. He had been aware that someone was with him, but in his semiconscious state, the identity of the person was of secondary importance to the cooling compress on his fever-flushed face. Not until that evening when she brought him in some chicken broth Freda had prepared did Jed recognize her.

His verbal abuse left her in little doubt that if he had the strength, he would have thrown her out of the house. Elizabeth accepted his sarcasm with forced silence, telling her bleeding heart that it was the result of the fever. She only partially believed it. He didn't want her there and she was a fool to stay, but she did.

There were moments in the succeeding two days when he was completely lucid and others when he succumbed to bouts of delirium, mumbling things that made no sense to Elizabeth. Sometimes she guessed that it had to do with his childhood, but mostly he seemed to refer to the time he had spent in the Pacific and South-east Asia.

Once he had called her name. She had slipped her hand over his, feeling his fingers tighten so she couldn't pull free.

'I'm here, Jed,' she had said in an aching whisper of love.

'You shouldn't be,' he had murmured huskily, trying to open the fever-weighted lids of his eyes. 'Why won't you go away?'

'Sssh, you must rest.' Elizabeth had bit into her lip to hold back the sob of despair.

'Leave me alone,' Jed had sighed, turning his head away from her on the pillow, but not relinquishing his grip on her hand. Stirring restlessly, he exclaimed with unexpected forcefulness, 'It's so damned hot! Doesn't anybody on this damned island own a fan?' And Elizabeth realized he was delirious again.

'He's out of it again, is he?' Kurt's voice had claimed Elizabeth's attention. He was standing in the doorway with Freda, fresh linen in her arms. 'I thought I'd give you two girls a hand changing the sheets.'

'I'll warn you, Kurt, Jed isn't very co-operative,' Elizabeth had cautioned with a sigh, twisting her hand free from Jed.

And he hadn't been co-operative, fighting the hands that removed the sweat-stained sheets from beneath

146

him to replace them with dry, hurling profanities at them indiscriminately. Finally when they had him tucked back in, he had seemed to collapse with exhaustion.

'He's hardly the model patient, is he?' Freda had breathed in deeply.

'I'm sorry,' Elizabeth had shaken her head wearily as they went out of the room.

'Don't be sorry,' Kurt had insisted. 'You certainly could never have managed him on your own, and I don't think Mrs. Carrel would have been of much help to you.'

Elizabeth had smiled, acknowledging silently the truth of his words. She doubted if she would have been able to manhandle Jed even in his weakened condition. Assistance from her mother-in-law would have been minimal at best. She had a very low tolerance of sick people, making her duty visits as she had done with Jed, but never staying any longer than propriety dictated.

'How about some iced tea on the porch before we turn in?' Kurt had suggested.

'It's a grand idea,' Freda had agreed. 'There's a pitcher full in the refrigerator. Would you fix a glass for Liza and me?' She had begun using Jed's nickname for Elizabeth. Without the faintly mocking undertones, Elizabeth hadn't objected.

'For my sister, anything,' Kurt had agreed laughingly, leaving the two girls to make their own way to the porch.

Leaning against one of the wooden porch-roof supports, Elizabeth had gazed at the evening stars sprinkled over the night sky. 'How long do you think it will last, Freda? Doctor Miles said only a few days, but it's already been three days.'

'His fever should be breaking soon.' Freda had curled on to the porch swing, tucking her legs beneath her. 'You love him very much, don't you?'

Elizabeth had swung around, a denial forming on her lips. Then she had sighed. 'Yes,' she had answered simply.

Freda hadn't offered any words of hope or confided anything that Jed might have said to her or Kurt. If she had, Elizabeth doubted if she would have believed her. She didn't think anyone knew what Jed felt, nor was he the type to let something slip.

There was an invisible clasping of hands between Elizabeth and Freda, cementing the friendship that had been steadily growing each hour they had spent together. Elizabeth had not realized how much she had missed the nonsensical talk with another girl, the exchanging of ideas whether on cooking or clothes or world politics without any attempt to impress the other with their intellectual prowess. If she had gained nothing else, she knew she had acquired a true friend.

Staring at the ceiling above her bed, Elizabeth waited for sleep to steal upon her, but her mind refused to stop reliving the happenings of the past three days. Restlessly, she thumped her pillow to relieve the tension, turning on her side and this time gazing at the sleeping figure of her daughter in the next bed. It was no use, she thought dejectedly. She simply

148

was not going to fall asleep as long as her mind kept racing about with thoughts of Jed.

A quilted housecoat lay at the foot of her bed. Slipping quietly from beneath the covers so as not to disturb Amy, Elizabeth slid her feet into the slippers at her bedside and picked up the housecoat. She would take a couple of minutes to check on Jed, she decided, then warm some milk in the kitchen. Wasn't that the old-fashioned cure-all for insomnia? she smiled at herself.

The yard light streamed through Jed's window, illuminating his tossing and turning figure. The blankets were thrown off, exposing the naked expanse of his bronzed chest. His pajama bottoms looked a paler blue in the dim light as Elizabeth hurried quietly into the room to draw the covers around him again. His skin was burning to the touch. Taking the ever-present cloth from the wash basin, she wiped the streaming perspiration from his unconsciously frowning face.

The fever was peaking. Cradling his head in her arms, Elizabeth pressed the water glass to his dry lips, letting the liquid trickle into his mouth. Directed by instinct, she kept repeating the procedure, first wiping the perspiration away, then giving him small swallows of water. Her heart cried out at her inability to do more to ease his discomfort as he continued to moan and toss. Her arms began to ache, her muscles throbbed with the constant repetition of her actions. She lost all perception of the minutes ticking by. It never once occurred to her to waken Freda.

Elizabeth didn't notice the exact moment when his fever broke. Suddenly she realized the frown had left his face and the restless turnings had ceased. His lean cheeks were still warm but without the fiery heat that had burned her hand. It was over. Jed was actually sleeping. With a trembling sound that was both a sigh and a sob, she collapsed wearily in the rocking chair beside his bed. She would sit here for a few minutes, she told herself, and let her aching muscles relax. It was for certain she wouldn't need any milk now, she decided with a wry smile. That was the last thing she remembered.

The next thing was the shooting pains in her neck. When she tried to move, they travelled down her spine. She frowned in protest, not wanting to move again, but the stiffness of her muscles demanded it. Slowly, unwillingly, Elizabeth opened her eyes, as the awareness of her surroundings gradually sank in and she awoke.

The sun was well up in the sky with no traces of the golden pink of dawn. Jed was sleeping peacefully, the stubble of a three-day beard growth darkening the lean jaw. The sallow look was gone from his face and there was no gleam of perspiration on his forehead. He was all right. A faint smile of relief touched her lips.

Arching her back to flex away the rigidity, Elizabeth began to gently rub the crook in her neck, the painful result of sleeping in the rocking chair the better part of the night. She still felt tired, but there was little point in going to bed at this hour. As she pushed herself out of the chair, her gaze shifted to the bed. Jed was watching her. The glaze of fever was gone, his eyes cat-gold and piercingly thorough in their appraisal.

'Didn't anyone ever tell you that chairs weren't made to sleep in?' His mouth quirked cynically at the corners.

Elizabeth opened her mouth to protest, her heart skipping beats, but the bedroom door was opened, effectively silencing her words. Freda stuck her head inside, glancing in surprise at Elizabeth, then to Jed. A smile spread across her face.

'Well, I see you've made it back to the land of reality.' Genuine welcome warmed her face. 'You must be starving, Jed. I'll bring you a tray.'

'Don't bother.' He rolled on to his back, his lazily alert gaze releasing Elizabeth to focus on his hostess. 'Elizabeth will be out shortly. She can fix it.'

The other girl raised a curious eyebrow, looked briefly at Elizabeth's astonished expression, then shrugged her agreement. The closing of the door brought an end to her initial confusion.

'I had planned to shower and change,' she told him tartly, resenting his autocratic command that she should wait on him when she had stayed up half the night taking care of him.

The complacent expression on his face didn't vary. 'I thought you were enjoying your role as the angel of mercy.' With disconcerting ease, Jed switched from mockery. 'How long have I been out?'

'Three days.'

'Three days?' He rubbed his hand over his chin, his beard scraping the palm. 'I hope I didn't bore you with

151

recollections of my lurid past.' He smiled ruefully.

'You mumbled too much,'' Elizabeth replied quietly and honestly. 'When we could understand your rambling, it didn't make any sense.'

His hooded glance had a measuring look about it, as if he was judging the truthfulness of her answer. She met it squarely without flinching, knowing how she would dislike having the privacy of her thoughts paraded before others without being aware of it.

'I remember telling you to leave. Why didn't you?'

Her love for him made that question difficult to answer honestly, so she settled for a half-truth. 'It wouldn't have been fair to let Freda and Kurt shoulder the entire responsibility of caring for you. They had their own work to do.'

'So a sense of duty compelled you to stay. Very commendable,' he murmured dryly.

'I was worried about you!' Elizabeth declared in despairing anger.

'I'm touched,' Jed mocked, reaching for the pitcher of water on the bedside table and nearly knocking it over when he tried to turn it around to grasp the handle.

'Let me do that,' she sighed, taking the pitcher from him and filling the glass with water. Automatically she sat on the edge of the bed, cupping the back of his head with her hand and raising the glass to his mouth. She didn't consider he no longer needed her help. 'The next time you get one of these attacks,' she flashed, still smarting from his amused sarcasm that jeered her nursing efforts, 'remind me to hire some thick-skinned nurse to take care of you. This is the last time I'll sit up half the night and be rewarded with abuse and ingratitude from you!'

The glass was jerked from his lips the instant he indicated he was satisfied. Before she could rise angrily to her feet, his arm circled her waist to keep her at his side.

'I'm sorry.' His tawny eyes were sparkling over the mutinous set of her mouth. 'I didn't say thank you, did I?'

'No, you didn't,' she retorted, her stomach churning in reaction to his touch. Her hands were unable to remove his pinning arm.

'There you go again, becoming all haughty and disdainful, just like you did the first day I came back.' The grooves around his mouth deepened mockingly. 'I often wondered whether you were more afraid I would steal the family valuables or you.'

'You looked like a tramp. How was I supposed to react?' Elizabeth challenged coolly.

'You were all cool and sophisticated then, too," Jed continued with thoughtful amusement. 'Snapping out orders and warnings with all the arrogant pride of a true Carrel. The beautiful, fragile creature with the green eyes seemed to have disappeared, the one I remember as being intimidated by the Carrel name and frightened that she might not be good enough for the favorite son. That's probably why I kept scratching the surface to see if any traces remained of the girl I remembered. Your veneer of sophistication is very thin, Liza.'

'Jed,' she gulped out her protest as he drew her down to the pillow, 'you've been ill.'

His face was only tantalizing inches from hers. 'I don't feel ill.' He smiled at the shaky breath she drew. 'Perhaps in view of my weakened condition you should humor me.'

His hand traced the outline of her face, his thumb lightly brushing her lips before his hand settled on the curve of her neck. At the moment, Elizabeth was certain that she was the one in the weakened condition. Her resistance, what little there was, was melting as swiftly as the wax beneath a candlewick.

'I know a man isn't supposed to ask, but do you object if I kiss you?' Jed moved his head closer to hers, hesitating a breath away from her lips.

'No.' It was almost a moan.

'You've objected all the other times,' he murmured against her mouth. 'This time I wanted you to want it as much as I do.'

Still he teased with feathery light kisses until her lips throbbed with the need for his possession. She wound her arms around his neck, trying to draw him down to her, but he held himself away easily.

'I don't understand you,' Elizabeth whispered achingly.

His beard scraped her cheek, then her throat, as he nuzzled the sensitive area of her neck, sending shivers of tortuous bliss down her spine. He slid his hand into her robe, letting it caress her waist and hips through the thin material of her nightgown.

'Please, Jed,' she begged shamelessly. 'Don't torment me this way.' Her eyes filled with longing.

'I wonder if you know the meaning of the word,' he muttered, nipping sharply at her ear lobe and drawing a gasp of pain mixed with pleasure.

But her plea succeeded as his head raised, his darkening hazel-gold eyes focusing on her trembling lips. The seconds stretched together again while he deliberately waited. The moan that escaped her lips when he finally claimed them was involuntary, an unwilling admission of the completeness of her surrender. The kiss was thorough and complete, his sensual technique without fault. The wildfire raging through her blood made any other man's touch seem like a tiny match flame by comparison.

Yet her hunger for his embrace was insatiable. She arched toward him when he pulled away. He stayed just tantalizing out of her reach, teasing her relentlessly. His heart was thudding as madly as hers. She could feel it beneath the palm of her hand resting against his chest.

'Were you worried about me?' he demanded huskily.

'You know I was,' she whispered.

'Why?' He pushed her back against the pillow, pinning her there with the weight of his body. 'Why should you care?'

'Because,' lamely evading his question.

'Why?' Jed persisted gruffly, aware of the way his touch was destroying her inhibitions. When she didn't answer, his fingers dug into her shoulder bone. 'Say it!' he snapped.

155

Gazing into his eyes, Elizabeth saw that the flecks were not malleable gold. Only the color was there to conceal his iron control, metallic and unyielding. Her viridescent eyes glistened with the tears she knew she would eventually shed.

'Because,' her voice quivered uncontrollably, 'I love you, Jed. I love you.'

There was a gleam of triumph in his eyes before his mouth obliterated all conscious thought with a hungry passion. Before she had only felt his virile surface warmth. Now she was consumed by the fiery urgency of his kiss. Not even when she had guessed how deeply Jed affected her had she ever dreamed that she would know this exploding joy.

CHAPTER NINE

'WOULD it be an understatement to say that you've recovered, Jed?'

The sarcastically contemptuous voice was the hiss of the serpent in the garden. The spitting tongue brought an abrupt end to the kiss that had been progressively leading to more than a passionate embrace. Elizabeth struggled red-faced to her feet, quickly knotting the sash of her robe, while Jed rolled on to his back, barely perturbed by the interruption.

'You have a lousy sense of timing, Mother,' he murmured dryly.

The smoldering outrage was evident in the disdainful set of Rebecca Carrel's features, but her control was as strong as her son's. She flicked a cutting glance at Elizabeth, showing disgust for her abandoned behavior.

'That is a matter of opinion, Jed,' his mother responded coldly. 'You appear quite healthy to me. I don't see that you'll require Elizabeth's presence any longer. We can put an end to this nursing nonsense.'

'She was about to fix my breakfast,' he said with a crooked, humorous smile.

'She is not a servant!' Rebecca snapped. 'Have that farm girl get your meal.'

Elizabeth stiffened resentfully. 'Freda is busy. If you'll excuse me, I'll get the breakfast.' The nervous smoothing of her mussed black curls stopped as she moved past her mother-in-law to the door.

'While you're gone, you'd better check on your child,' was the waspish response. 'When I came in, she was playing with those dirty puppies, letting them paw and climb all over her. She looked as filthy as a beggar child!'

'A little dirt won't harm her,' Elizabeth retorted.

'Perhaps you have forgotten she has a piano lesson this morning. It may have also slipped your mind that she missed the last one for' — there was a deliberate pause in the condescending reminder — 'unexplained reasons.'

'The reasons were personal.' The tilt of Elizabeth's chin dared Rebecca to inquire further. 'And I will decide if it's essential that she keep this one.'

'I don't know what possible excuse you can offer Mrs. Banks. Not now that Jed has recovered.'

'Since I'm paying for the lessons, I wasn't aware that I needed an excuse!' Elizabeth was shaking with uncontrollable anger as she stepped into the hall, slamming the bedroom door behind her.

She took her time in the shower and dressed with equal slowness. She couldn't recall a time that she had talked back to her mother-in-law, and certainly never so rudely. The only twinge of remorse she felt was for losing her temper, not for the things she had said. She didn't venture out of her room until she heard Rebecca's car start up in the drive.

Freda had left a note on the kitchen table telling Elizabeth that she was out in the garden. Amy was in the porch swing, crooning to a sleeping puppy in her lap. Doubting that Jed's stomach could take a sudden jolt of solid food, Elizabeth prepared a bowl of hot cereal, toast and cocoa and carried it into his room on a tray.

Setting the tray across his lap, she walked silently to the window. It seemed incredible that a short time ago she had been in his arms, pledging her love with each breath she drew. Jed had barely glanced at her when she entered the room, remote again, withdrawn into that aloofness she had never been able to penetrate.

'You're very quiet all of a sudden,' he commented.

'There's nothing left for me to say,' Elizabeth shrugged, letting the curtain fall and turning toward him, her look unconsciously reminding him that it was his turn.

'You should have time to pack your things before Amy's lesson. Freda can drive you to the house or take you on into town if you'd rather.' He was sipping his cocoa with crushing unconcern.

'Is that what you want? For me to leave?' she asked in a choked voice that was both stiff and proud.

He held her gaze for a long moment. 'It isn't what I want, but it's what I'm willing to settle for,' he replied evenly.

'What do you want?' Elizabeth stared at the fingers twisting and untwisting in front of her, surprised to discover that they belonged to her.

'I thought I'd made that plain.' He tilted his head

curiously to one side, studying her intently. 'I want you.'

Not 'I love you' or 'I want to marry you,' but simply 'I want you,' as if she were a possession that he had coveted for a long time and intended to own.

'I'll start packing now.' Dispiritedly she turned away, her eyes downcast to conceal the gathering tears.

'Liza? What's the matter?' Jed demanded as she started towards the door. 'Liza!' he called to her again, angrily this time when she continued to ignore him. 'Dammit! Answer me!'

She hesitated in the doorway. 'I'm tired, Jed.' It was true. She felt emotionally drained.

The tears slipping from her lashes were a defense mechanism against the tension that had been building since last night. She didn't actually cry, but it took her a long time to pack her and Amy's things. The steady stream of tears kept blurring her vision.

Later Freda apologized for not warning Elizabeth of Rebecca's arrival, but Elizabeth dismissed it. 'There was no harm done. She didn't interrupt anything.' At least, nothing that didn't need to be interrupted, but she found she couldn't confide that to Freda.

Her fragile composure wouldn't survive another visit to Jed's room, so she left it to Freda to let him know that she had actually gone. Only a few grumbles were sounded from Amy's quarters, not any more than she usually offered on the days of her piano lesson. Elizabeth chose not have Freda take her own car. Too much time in her friend's company would loosen her tongue, and until she had time to think things through on her own, that was something she didn't want.

The instant they returned from Amy's lesson and stepped into the entrance hall, Elizabeth recognized the cause for the cloud of dread that had been following her. Rebecca was waiting for her, looking every inch the sophisticated matron of society with her perfectly coiffed silver hair and dusty-rose dress. This morning's incident was not going to escape without comment.

'There are cookies and milk in the kitchen for you, Amy. You may practise after you have eaten,' Rebecca smiled amiably at her granddaughter. Elizabeth started to counter her orders out of sheer stubbornness until she met the coal-hard chips of her mother-in-law's eyes. The confrontation was to occur now, she realized. It was better that it did not begin in front of Amy. 'I've put the coffee service in Franklin's study so we won't disturb Amy,' the older woman informed her when Amy had left them.

The sarcastic brittleness of this morning was absent from Rebecca's voice, but Elizabeth wasn't deceived by the pleasant tone. Tight-lipped, she walked to the closed study door. Postponing this moment would be futile. Silently she endured her mother-in-law's quiet courtesy, accepting the cup of coffee that was handed her, aware all the while that the stage had been set by Rebecca for this meeting. The calmness of her voice, the coffee, and the privacy of the study was calculated to inspire trust and confidence.

A tray of ladyfingers was offered to Elizabeth, but she waved it aside, setting the untouched cup of coffee onto the tray. 'Please, Rebecca,' she said evenly, 'let's dispense with the niceties. Say whatever it is that you brought me in here to say.'

Rebecca set her own cup down, folding her hands primly in her lap and falsely hesitating for an instant. Her head was tipped downward as if to study the clear polish on her nails.

'First of all,' the silver-gray head was raised to meet the impassive greennesss of Elizabeth's gaze, 'I want to apologize for my behavior this morning. I was shocked. It was never my intention to interfere in your personal life or usurp your authority with Amy. I spoke in haste and without thinking, and I'm sorry.'

'Was that all?' Elizabeth knew the stiffness of her attitude and her failure to soften in response to the apology disconcerted Rebecca, but she concealed it admirably.

'No.' Rebecca rose to her feet, walking away from Elizabeth as if plagued by an uncertainty how to proceed. 'I have heard the rumors that — that you and Jed were interested in each other. For the most part I discounted it as idle gossip. I never doubted for an instant that Jed would make advances toward you. He has always pursued the opposite sex and with considerable success.

She glanced over her shoulder to see the effect her comments were making, but Elizabeth deliberately kept her face devoid of any expression and waited for Rebecca to continue.

'I have never understood why the wastrels of this world hold so much appeal for women,' her mother-in-law sighed, then smiled. 'Perhaps it is because at birth they were endowed with virile looks and charm so that intelligence and ambition were wasted on them. They have no need for them. They can get what they want without them. Jed is like that — he exudes an aura of danger and excitement that make women feel deliciously sinful. His father and I recognized that early in his teenage years. It was a source of constant concern.'

Rebecca resumed her chair opposite Elizabeth, leaning forward in an earnest, confiding manner, anxiety darkening her brown eyes further. Her hands were clasped in front of her in a plea for understanding.

'Now, my concern is for you, Elizabeth,' she murmured fervidly. 'I foolishly never warned you about Jed. I should have given thought to the fact that you are young and in need of physical gratification.'

The way Rebecca was speaking made Elizabeth feel unclean. She could maintain her silence no longer, she must speak.

'It's not lust I feel for Jed, Rebecca. 'It's love,' she said quietly. 'I did not intend to fall in love with him. I tried to pretend myself that it was only physical attraction, but it wasn't. I love him, and I'm not ashamed of it.'

Surprisingly there wasn't any disapproving outburst, simply a softly spoken question. 'Does Jed know this?'

'Yes.'

'I see.' Rebecca didn't appear surprised by the admission. 'And what are your plans?'

'There are no plans,' Elizabeth answered. The faint I-thought-as-much expression forced her to add in defense, 'Jed has been ill.'

'He will ask you to go away with him.' It was a statement made with assurance, not a question.

'Did he say that?' The wary question was out before Elizabeth could stop it.

'No.' Rebecca studied her hands. 'It's more of a guess on my part, an accurate one, I believe. When he does,' she glanced up, forcing Elizabeth to meet her gaze, 'what will you do?'

'I'll go with him. I love him, Rebecca,' Elizabeth said firmly.

Her mother-in-law sighed and leaned back in her chair. 'I won't pretend that I have any right to tell you what to do. You're quite old enough to make your own decisions. But I feel compelled to point out some things to you. Jed is thirty-two years old. He doesn't have a career or a job. He doesn't live anywhere, so he has no house or apartment, not even a car. Only a token sum was left to him in Franklin's will, so he has no money either. I don't mean to imply that these things are important if you love someone,' Rebecca hastened to add in response to the seething anger tightening the line of Elizabeth's mouth. 'I'm asking you to consider these things for Amy's sake, for her future. It's true that you do receive a monthly sum from her trust fund, but it would never support a household. However much you may believe you love Jed, you must consider her welfare. Think about what I've said. Please, Elizabeth.'

With a gentle smile, Rebecca rose and left the room. Elizabeth sat silently. She had made no response because there was none to make. There was little consolation in recognizing that the speech and its delivery had been carefully rehearsed to achieve the reaction she was now experiencing. The request had been logical and reasonable and impossible to argue against. Elizabeth's vulnerable spot was Amy. Rebecca hadn't wasted time with meaningless slashes but had gone straight for the jugular vein.

Blindly Elizabeth had never looked ahead — perhaps because she wasn't convinced that Jed wanted her in more than a physical sense. If he did, what would she do then? It was so impossible to cross bridges when they hadn't been reached.

Late that afternoon, she telephoned the farm to see how Jed was. Secretly she was hoping that he would be up and she would have a chance to talk to him. The shadows of uncertainty were becoming too much. Freda answered the phone.

'How's Jed?' Elizabeth inquired with what she hoped was the right tone of interest.

'Fine. He had a big lunch and went to sleep. I think he intends to sleep the clock round. It's probably the best thing for him,' Freda answered brightly.

'Yes, you're probably right,' Elizabeth agreed reluctantly.

'Will you be coming over this evening?'

'I don't think so. I only wanted to be sure he was all right.' There was no point in going over. As always, it seemed to be Jed's move. 'I have some things to catch up here at the house.'

'I'll tell him you called.'

'Yes, Goodbye, Freda.' Slowly Elizabeth replaced the receiver.

Strangely, the hours passed swiftly. It was something of a start when Elizabeth realized that two full days and the morning of a third had gone by since her leaving the Reisner farm. The tension had increased rather than eased. Uncertainty and indecision trailed her wherever she went.

Jed was recovering quickly, or so Freda told her. Elizabeth hadn't heard a word from him. He hadn't given Freda any indication when he would be returning home, which didn't surprise Elizabeth. Something told her she could rely on Jed to come home when she least expected him.

Stepping to the raised kitchen window, she glanced out, spying Amy beside the patio table where her play cups and saucers were spread out.

'It's almost time for lunch, Amy. You'd better get washed up,' she called. 'We'll have it in the kitchen since your grandmother isn't here.'

Absently Elizabeth heard the french doors open and close and the sound of water running in the downstairs bathroom wash basin. She ladled the soup into bowls and uncovered the plate of sandwiches and set it on the table.

A carton of milk was in her hand when a deep voice

asked, 'Will lunch stretch to three?' She started.

Quickly she sat the carton on the counter before she dropped it, boundless joy surging through her veins. She didn't need to turn around to know that Ned had come back, when she had least expected him. Commanding her hands to stop trembling, she took a third glass from the cupboard and filled it with milk.

'Of course it will, Jed,' she responded warmly, sliding a glance behind her as he approached. 'You're looking fine.'

"Completely recovered.' He stopped beside her, tawny gold eyes regarding her intently.

Hypnotically she returned the look. There was nothing about him to suggest that he had been ill. His vigorously masculine features showed no signs of tiredness or strain. Vitality abounded in his watchful stillness.

'You look wonderful.' There was a breathless catch in her voice.

His eyebrow raised mockingly. 'So do you,' he murmured.

'Oh, boy!' Tomato soup, my favorite!' Amy announced, sliding on to one of the chairs.

Jed smiled. 'I think someone is hungry! I suppose we should eat.'

Elizabeth swallowed and nodded. 'Sit down. I'll get another place setting for myself.'

Food was the last thing on her mind. Inwardly she crossed her fingers that Jed had been implying the same thing. It did little good to tell herself to remain calm, that all the unknowns hadn't vanished simply because Jed was back. She went through the motions of eating her soup and nibbling at a sandwich.

'Amy tells me she has a birthday party to go to this afternoon,' Jed commented.

Elizabeth frowned bewilderedly. 'When did she tell you that?'

'Out on the patio.'

'I didn't see you there,' she breathed.

'I know.' The grooves around his mouth deepened in silent amusement. 'What are you doing this afternoon?'

'I have a meeting.' There was no attempt to disguise the disappointment in her voice as she stared unseeingly at her soup. 'I'm the secretary. I have to attend.'

'I see,' he answered evenly, not trying to dissuade her as he switched the topic to the birthday party, asking Amy about her friends.

While Elizabeth cleared the table of the luncheon dishes, she sent Amy upstairs to dress for her party, reminding her to take her swimming suit and towel since part of the activities included a visit to the public swimming pool. Jed disappeared into another part of the house. There was no sign of him when she went upstairs to change for her meeting. But he was in the front hallway with Amy when she came back downstairs.

'Do you have any objections if I act as chauffeur?' he asked.

'None at all.' Elizabeth shook her head. Rebecca had the other car, which only left hers to provide him transportation. Obviously he had somewhere to go.

Conversation was minimal during the drive into town. Most of it was Amy's chatter about the party. No matter how many glances Elizabeth stole at Jed's profile, there was nothing in his impassive expression to indicate that he felt her disappointment.

The old familiar depression settled around her shoulders. Fortunately Amy was too excited about her party to notice the sadness in her mother's smile when they left her at the house of the birthday girl. Elizabeth stared out the window, wondering what she could say to end the silence.

'Turn left at the next corner. The Hansons' house is the third one on the right-hand side.' The directions were given reluctantly.

But Jed drove straight through the intersection without stopping.

'I meant that corner,' Elizabeth pointed behind them. 'You'll have to go around the block.'

'I know which corner you mean.' Jed glanced at her briefly and continued through the second intersection that would have taken them back in a round-about way.

'I have to go to the meeting,' she reminded him with a frown.

Slowing the car, he turned it into the curbside of the street, stopping it but not switching off the engine as he twisted in the seat to look at her.

'Which would you rather do? Go to that stupid meeting or come with me?' he asked with thinning patience.

'I'd rather come with you —' Elizabeth began sighing in frustration.

'That settles it, then.' He put the car in gear and pulled back into the street.

'But, Jed —'

'I don't know about you, but I don't want to wait until tonight,' he said firmly. 'We've postponed our talk long enough. Don't you agree?'

'Yes,' Elizabeth surrendered, not caring one whit about the meeting she was supposed to attend.

His slow smile seemed to reach and almost physically touch her. It was a heady sensation and very enjoyable. That bridge she was worried about was coming closer. She still didn't know whether she was going to cross it or not, but she had to see it. She would never be able to come to a decision until she did.

CHAPTER TEN

AFTER Jed had expressed a desire to talk, there was silence in the car. He continued driving through town and into the outskirts. It wasn't the road that would take them back to the house. Elizabeth couldn't guess what destination he had in mind. The last place she would have thought of was the small municipal airport outside town, but that was where Jed turned.

'What are we doing here?' She glanced curiously at Jed as he pulled in beside the three cars parked outside the flight office and switched off the engine.

'You might say this is my old stamping grounds.' He opened the door and stepped out, walking around to her side, smiling at her slightly bewildered expression. 'I spent more time here than I ever did in school or at home, outside of Kurt's.'

Elizabeth silently digested that piece of information, studying the happy and contented look about him as he gazed at the few buildings that constituted the Carrelville airport. A little puff of breeze was trying to fill the orange windsock.

'Do you mean' — she asked hesitantly — 'that you used to fly?'

Jed glanced down, the contented smile curving his mouth. His arm circled her shoulders as he turned her in the direction of the flight office. She was surprised.

'Come one, I'll show you,' he said. Entering the flight office, he lifted the counter and led Elizabeth into the hall leading to the back, private offices. Her puzzled frown deepened at his easy familiarity. He opened one of the doors leading off the hall. 'This is where Sam hangs up his shirt-tails.'

'Shirt-tails?' she repeated, as she walked in ahead of him.

'It's a ceremony that all prospective pilots go through,' Jed explained. 'After a student makes his first solo flight, his instructor cuts off his shirt-tail and hangs it up. It's referred to as "clipping his tail feathers." ' He led her to the wall that was patch-worked with strips of cloth of every pattern and color. Those are mine,' he pointed.

On a strip of pale blue material was scrawled Jed's name and the date. Elizabeth made a swift mental calculation and looked at him in surprise.

'You were only sixteen!' she breathed.

Jed chuckled softly. 'I had the devil's own time per-suading Sam to teach me without my parent's per-mission. He knew if there was any accident, Dad would come down on him like a ton of bricks.'

'You mean they don't know?'

'Eventually they found out. Somebody from town saw me landing a plan and mentioned it to Dad. I was only a few hours away from getting my license when Dad stopped my allowance. Fortunately Sam let me work out the rest of the money. In college, I wanted to major in aerodynamics, but Dad wouldn't hear of it.

As long as he was paying the tuition, he insisted I had to take up law, like all the rest of the Carrels. His mouth twisted bitterly before he shook away the memory. 'Come on, let's walk.'

From the flight office, they wandered into the hangar area. In one of the sheds, a man in overalls was working on a plane. When he spotted them, he cupped his hands to his mouth and called out:

'Do you want me to roll out the twin for you, Jed?'

'Not today, Sam,' Jed waved the offer aside.

Elizabeth was nestled under the crook of his arm. She tilted her head back to gaze into his face, her heart singing a bit at the warmth with which his tawny eyes returned her look.

'Have you been out here often since you came back?' she asked.

'You surely didn't think I spent all that time at the Reisner farm, did you?' he grinned.

'I didn't know where you were or who you were with.' A faint pink of self-consciousness glowed in her cheeks as she averted her gaze.

'But you were imagining,' Jed teased, tightening his arm around her shoulders as they ducked beneath the wing of a tied-down plane. 'If I disappear on you some day after we're married, don't check the golf course. Just go to the nearest airport and I'll probably be there.'

Elizabeth stopped abruptly, her gaze freezing on his face and her heart nearly stopping altogether. The light breeze lifted the tobacco brown hair that fell over his forehead, revealing his puzzled frown.

'What's wrong?' he asked.

'What — What did you just say?' she murmured.

'I said —' Then Jed stopped and laughed softly at himself. 'I didn't intend to propose to you in just that way.'

'Do you mean you want to marry me?' Elizabeth whispered, not quite believing it yet.

'What did you think I wanted?' Jed smiled gently as he turned her into his arms, locking his hands behind her back.

Closing her eyes, she leaned her head against his chest, feeling his lips moving in a tender caress against her hair. 'I was afraid to think.' Her voice trembled. 'There was always the chance that all you wanted was an affair.'

He lifted her chin with his finger. 'Would you have settled for that?'

'If that was all I could have,' she answered truthfully, the love in her heart pouring out of her glistening eyes.

Possession marked the kiss that bruised her lips. It was a hard, short kiss as if to punish her for doubting the depth of his emotion. There was a determined glitter in his eyes when he lifted his head.

'Now you know I mean to have you for ever,' Jed saif firmly. 'I knew you belonged to me that night Jeremy brought you home.'

At this moment, Elizabeth didn't want to think, only feel. She wanted this moment to stretch out for an eternity of time, to glory in his love for the rest of her life. But she wouldn't do that. Not yet, anyway.

'What . . . about Amy?' She stared at his open shirt collar for an instant before lifting anxious eyes to his face.

A bemused smile spread across his mouth. 'Amy is a part of you. What did you think I was going to do? Tell you to get rid of her?' he laughed with a trace of bewilderment.

'I . . . wasn't sure,' Elizabeth faltered again.

'Now you know,' he answered patiently, lifting her chin when she would have averted her head. 'You haven't said whether you'll marry me, Liza.'

'Yes, but —'

Jed stiffened. 'The answer is never "yes" when there's a "but" attached to it. The watchful and withdrawn look removed the warmth from his gaze as he studied her guilty expression intently. 'What's bothering you?'

There was no resistance when she pulled away from his embrace. 'Jed, if it was only me that was involved, I'd . . . I'd marry you in a minute.' Nervously she brushed the hair away from her face. 'I wouldn't care if we lived in the back room of some airport or a grass hut on a beach as long as I'd be with you. But I have to consider Amy's welfare.'

'What are you asking? Whether I can keep you in the style you've become accustomed to?' Jed demanded tightly.

'No,' she protested.

'What is it then? Do you measure the amount of faith you can have in a man by the size of his bank balance?'

Elizabeth's stomach churned at the bitterness in his expression. 'What kind of a mother would I be, Jed, if I wasn't concerned how our marriage might affect Amy?' she asked quietly, lowering her chin so she wouldn't have to meet his accusing gaze.

'You might have sufficient trust in me to know that I would take care of you both,' he answered grimly.

'I understand why you feel hurt,' she replied in a choked voice. 'You have every right to feel that way. But please understand the way I feel. I trust you with my life, Jed. And Amy trusts me with hers.'

He turned away from her, raking his fingers through the thick brownness of his hair. A controlled fury darkened his eyes when he glanced at her.

'What will it take to make you decide whether you'll marry me or not?' he snapped.

'Just a little time,' Elizabeth murmured. 'I didn't expect you to propose. I'd . . . I'd like to think it over. Oh, Jed, I love you desperately — you must believe that.' Her chin quivered. 'I just don't want to give you an answer now that we both might regret.'

'I'll never regret loving you.' He stared into the cloudless blue sky, his hands shoved deep in his pockets. 'If it's time you want, you have it.' He pulled a hand from his pocket and stretched it toward her, keys jingled from his fingers. 'Here, I'll find my own way home.'

'Jed —'

'I'd like to be alone, Elizabeth,' he interrupted sharply. 'I have a few things to think over, too.'

'I do love you,' she murmured achingly, unable to

shake the feeling that she had betrayed him as she clutched the keys tightly against her stomach.

His narrowed gaze slid to her. 'If I didn't believe that, I don't think I'd let you go.'

Slowly she turned and retraced her steps toward the car. The one time she had looked back she saw him walking in the opposite direction away from her. She felt miserable and sick inside.

At the car, she stopped and started to turn back. Her answer was yes. There was no other answer that she could possibly make. Without Jed, she would be an empty shell. She had already given him her heart and she couldn't take it back. Maybe Amy wouldn't have some of the material things that Elizabeth could give her now, but Amy would be a part of the happiness and love that she and Jed would share. And that was a priceless thing.

But she didn't run back to Jed as she wanted to. He had asked to be alone, and it was a request she felt she should respect. Besides, she didn't want him to think that her decision had been prompted by any sense of guilt. She would give him her answer the minute he arrived home. All she could do now was pray that he would accept the fact that she loved him and trusted him implicitly in everything.

Two hours later, Elizabeth was sitting at the piano picking out the tune of a popular love ballad. A gentle breeze dancing through the open French doors. The front door opened and closed. With her fingers resting soundlessly on the keys, she turned a nervously expectant smile toward the hall, lovelight glistening through the anxious green of her eyes. It was Rebecca who appeared in the archway.

'So this is where you are,' her mother-in-law said sharply. 'Mrs. Hanson said you weren't at the meeting today and that you didn't even bother to notify her that you wouldn't come. She said she phoned here but no one answered.'

'I wasn't here.' Elizabeth turned back to the piano. 'I was with Jed.'

There was an instant of alert silence before Rebecca murmured, 'I see.' She walked slowly into the room. 'Where is he now?'

Elizabeth's fingers absently began playing a soft melody to ease the tension that suddenly enveloped the room. 'At the airport.'

'He's leaving?' There was surprised disbelief in the question.

'No. No, he'll be back later,' Elizabeth assured her firmly, a faint smile touching the corners of her mouth.

'You sound very certain.'

'He has asked me to marry him. I told him I wanted to think it over.'

'That was very wise of you, my dear. I knew you were much too sensible to let your head be turned by a charming wastrel like my son. If you wish to remarry, you can certainly find a more suitable partner,' Rebecca declared complacently.

'I don't think you understood me. I didn't refuse Jed.' Elizabeth felt serenely calm as she met her mother-in-law's raised eyebrows. 'It's the things in life you don't do that you regret. In fact, I have decided to marry him. If I didn't marry Jed, I would regret it the rest of my life.'

'But what about Amy?'

'Amy will be well taken care of. We'll both see to that,' Elizabeth answered confidently.

'You can't live on love!' Rebecca declared. 'How on earth will he support the two of you when he doesn't have a job or money?'

'That's our concern, Rebecca.'

'You're being foolish! You can't —'

The telephone interrupted her with a shrill ring. Rebecca glared at it angrily before giving in to its summons and walking to answer it. Elizabeth smiled at the barely disguised impatience in her mother-in-law's voice when she picked up the receiver. Her decision was unshakable. There was nothing Rebecca could say that would make her change her mind.

'Long-distance? No, he isn't here,' Rebecca spoke sharply into the receiver. 'I do expect him later.'' — 'He has been ill for a few days. Perhaps that's why you weren't able to reach him.' — Elizabeth had been listening absently, curious who it was that was calling Jed long-distance, but not really paying too close attention until she heard the note of sharpened interest in her mother-in-law's voice. 'May I take a message for him?' — 'I am his mother.' — Quickly she began scribbling a message on the paper that was always kept beside the telephone, squinting at her writing without taking the time to get her glasses from her purse. 'The offer was from whom?' —'Yes, I have the amount.' —

'I will give him the message the minute he comes in.' Slowly Rebecca replaced the receiver on the hook, staring at the paper in front of her.

'Who was it?' Elizabeth asked, becoming more curious at her mother-in-law's puzzling behavior.

'It was from Jed's attorney in Honolulu. Jed's attorney,' she repeated as if she couldn't accept what she was saying. 'Some firm has just made an offer to buy his airline.'

'I don't understand,' Elizabeth frowned.

'I don't think I do either.' There was a short, disbelieving laugh from Rebecca. 'It seems Jed owns this company that flies cargo to the different islands in the Pacific and parts of the Asian mainland. Why didn't he tell us? Did you know?

'No, I had no idea.'

'He's,' Rebecca held out the paper as proof, ' a wealthy man. Oh, Elizabeth!' A smile broke across her face as she hurried quickly to take her daughter-in-law's hands in her own. 'Of course you must accept his proposal. I'll take care of all the arrangements for the wedding. It'll be a small affair, not too many —'

'I believe you have a message for me, Mother.' Jed's quiet voice slashed the air with the deadly silence of a rapier thrust.

The astonishment that had been on Elizabeth's face changed to horror as she whirled to see him standing in the French doors. The hardened look about his lean features confirmed her guess that he had overheard their conversation. The cat-gold eyes held her motionless, ignoring the gushings of his mother as she proclaimed how proud she was of him and how delighted she was about his engagement to Elizabeth.

A sob bubbled into Elizabeth's throat. He would never believe her now. She could never convince him that she had been willing to marry him before she found out that he more than had the means to support her and Amy. No matter what she said, he would always think that the phone call had influenced her decision.

With a muffled cry of pain, she broke free of his gaze, tears scalding her eyes and cheeks as she raced from the room. She heard him call her name, but it only increased her desire to flee. She loved him too deeply to endure the sting of his mockery at this moment. Fumbling with the front doorknob, she jerked it open, not bothering to close the door as she hurried down the sidewalk.

Before she could reach the car Rebecca had left in the driveway in front of the garage, a hand was biting into the soft flesh of her arm, bringing her flight to an abrupt halt and spinning her around so that her other arm was captured also. She struggled against the punishing grip.

'Let me go! Please, Jed, let me go,' she begged, twisting and turning her head so he couldn't see the tears streaming down her face.

But he was oblivious to her protests, pulling her rigid body against his and forcing her head back to receive his long, hard kiss. He kept on kissing her until she stopped resisting him and the love she couldn't deny. Only then did he release her lips, allowing her to bury her face in his chest. She felt utterly miserable.

'I know you'll never believe me.' Her sobs were muffled by his shirt. 'But I swear I'd decided to marry you before that phone call. At the airport, I started to go back to tell you, but you'd said you wanted to be alone and — Oh, you'll never believe me now!'

'Stop crying.' He shook her gently as he scolded her with mock gruffiness. 'I was on the patio.'

'I know you were.' Her voice throbbed with pain. 'And I know what you must think of me.'

'You don't understand.' Forcing her head up, he tenderly wiped the tears from her cheek. 'I heard everything. I was on the patio listening to you play the piano before Mother came home. You told her before the phone rang that you were going to marry me. I was on my way in to make you tell me that. I never guessed the call would be for me. I'd left Sam's number for my attorney, but unfortunately he forgot to give me the message. So you see, darling, I know you're telling the truth, that you're willing to marry me for richer, for poorer.'

'Oh, Jed,' Elizabeth gasped, her lashes fluttering shut for a second. 'I was so afraid —'

'I know, darling.' He folded her more tightly into his arm. 'Now I have to ask you to forgive me. I wasn't being fair when I kept the truth from you and demanded that you make a decision without knowing what kind of future, if any, I could offer you.'

'Why didn't you let anyone know?' she asked softly, her hands lovingly caressing his face. 'You should have been proud of your success.'

'It was foolish Carrel pride,' he smiled crookedly. 'I wanted to be welcomed for myself, not for my accomplishments. Kurt and Sam, my friends, were the only ones who could do that. And you, my lovely enchanting Liza.' He kissed her lightly. 'It seems I shall have some business to take care of in Hawaii. Would you object to spending our honeymoon there?'

'No,' she smiled happily.

'It'll be a month or more before we can come back.'

'Here?' Elizabeth frowned. 'With your mother?'

'Good lord, no!' Jed laughed. 'I may care for her, but I could never live in the same house with her.' His expression became more serious. 'We'll find a place of our own, ours and Amy's. Not too far away, because Mother needs us. She hasn't anything, darling, and we have so much. She needs our love.' He lowered his head to her lips. 'And I need yours.'

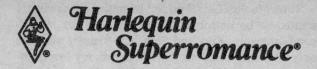

Harlequin Superromance®

Coming in August from
Harlequin Superromance
A new novel from the author of
BRIDGE TO YESTERDAY

IN GOOD TIME
By Muriel Jensen

A mad but cunning killer is stalking Paula Cornell.
Reluctantly, Paula must place her faith—and her life—
in the hands of bodyguard Dane Chandler, a man ten
years her junior.

In their secluded mountain hideout, Dane and Paula
fall in love. But unless Paula can overcome a tragedy
in her past, she will never be able to be the wife and
partner Dane needs her to be.

IN GOOD TIME
A story of hope and renewal
Superromance #512

IGT92

HARLEQUIN
Romance®

Harlequin's Ruth Jean Dale brings you THE TAGGARTS OF TEXAS!

Those Taggart men—strong, sexy and hard to resist...

There's Jesse James Taggart in **FIREWORKS!**
Harlequin Romance #3205 (July 1992)

And Trey Smith—he's **THE RED-BLOODED YANKEE!**
Harlequin Temptation #413 (October 1992)

Then there's Daniel Boone Taggart in **SHOWDOWN!**
Harlequin Romance #3242 (January 1993)

And finally the Taggarts who started it all—in **LEGEND!**
Harlequin Historical #168 (April 1993)

**Read all the Taggart romances!
Meet all the Taggart men!**

Available wherever Harlequin books are sold.   DALE-R

A PLACE IN HER HEART...

Somewhere deep in the heart of every grown woman is the little girl she used to be....

In September, October and November 1992, the world of childhood and the world of love collide in six very special romance titles. Follow these six special heroines as they discover the sometimes heart-wrenching, always heartwarming joy of being a Big Sister.

Written by six of your favorite Superromance authors, these compelling and emotionally satisfying romantic stories will earn a place in your heart!

SEPTEMBER 1992

#514 NOTHING BUT TROUBLE—Sandra James
#515 ONE TO ONE—Marisa Carroll

OCTOBER 1992

#518 OUT ON A LIMB—Sally Bradford
#519 STAR SONG—Sandra Canfield

NOVEMBER 1992

#522 JUST BETWEEN US—Debbi Bedford
#523 MAKE-BELIEVE—Emma Merritt

AVAILABLE WHEREVER
HARLEQUIN SUPERROMANCE
BOOKS ARE SOLD

WELCOME TO

The quintessential small town where everyone knows everybody else!

Finally, books that capture the pleasure of tuning in to your favorite TV show!

GREAT READING...GREAT SAVINGS...AND A FABULOUS FREE GIFT!

Each book set in Tyler is a self-contained love story; together, the twelve novels stitch the fabric of the community. The covers honor the old American tradition of quilting; each cover depicts a patch of the large Tyler quilt.

With Tyler you can receive a fabulous gift ABSOLUTELY FREE by collecting proofs-of-purchase found in each Tyler book. And use our special Tyler coupons to save on your next TYLER book purchase.

Join your friends at Tyler for the sixth book, SUNSHINE by Pat Warren, available in August.

When Janice Eber becomes a widow, does her husband's friend David provide more than just friendship?

Harlequin Superromance®

Come to where the West is still wild in a summer trilogy by Margot Dalton

Sunflower (#502—June 1992)
Robin Baldwin becomes the half owner of a prize
rodeo horse. But to take possession, she has to travel
the rodeo circuit with cowboy Matt Adams, living
with him in *very* close quarters!

Tumbleweed (#508—July 1992)
Until she met Scott Freeman, Lyle Callander was about
as likely to settle in one spot as tumbleweed in a
windstorm. But who *is* Scott? He's more than the
simple photographer he claims to be . . . much more.

Juniper (#511—August 1992)
Devil-may-care Buck Buchanan can ride a bucking
bronco or a Brahma bull. But can he win Claire
Tremaine, a woman who sets his heart on fire but
keeps her own as cold as ice?

**"I just finished reading *Under Prairie Skies* by
Margo Dalton and had to hide my tears from my
children. I loved it!"** —A reader